"So, this is where it happened?"

"Yes." She had a feeling that he had looked at crime scene photos to correspond with the precise location. "Aunt Veronica was murdered precisely where you're standing."

He stepped away, as if it was hallowed ground. "Sorry."

"It's okay. That was twenty years ago," she reminded him. "So, it's not nearly as unsettling to step or drive on the spot today." Never mind that the memories couldn't help but resurface by the very nature of his investigation.

"I suppose it wouldn't be." Scott gazed at the wooded area that Abby knew had filled out even more over the years. "Why don't you show me around inside?"

"Okay." She led him into the log cabin, wanting Scott to have a feel for the place that might somehow play on his mindset in trying to reconstruct the cold-blooded murder of her aunt Veronica and how the cold case might start to warm up.

To H. Loraine, the cherished love of my life and very best friend, whose support has been unwavering through the many wonderful years together. To my dear mother, Marjah Aljean, who gave me the tools to pursue my passions in life, including writing fiction for publication; and for my loving sister, Jacquelyn, who helped me become the person I am today along the way. To the loyal fans of my romance, mystery, suspense and thriller fiction published over the years.
Lastly, a nod goes out to my wonderful editors, Allison Lyons and Denise Zaza, for the great opportunity to lend my literary voice and creative spirit to the successful Harlequin Intrigue line.

COLD MURDER IN KOLTON LAKE

R. BARRI FLOWERS

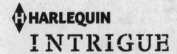

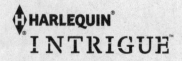

Recycling programs
for this product may
not exist in your area.

ISBN-13: 978-1-335-59081-7

Cold Murder in Kolton Lake

Copyright © 2024 by R. Barri Flowers

For questions and comments about the quality of this book, please contact us
at CustomerService@Harlequin.com.

TM and ® are trademarks of Harlequin Enterprises ULC.

Harlequin Enterprises ULC
22 Adelaide St. West, 41st Floor
Toronto, Ontario M5H 4E3, Canada
www.Harlequin.com

Printed in U.S.A.

R. Barri Flowers is an award-winning author of crime, thriller, mystery and romance fiction featuring three-dimensional protagonists, riveting plots, unexpected twists and turns, and heart-pounding climaxes. With an expertise in true crime, serial killers and characterizing dangerous offenders, he is perfectly suited for the Harlequin Intrigue line. Chemistry and conflict between the hero and heroine, attention to detail and incorporating the very latest advances in criminal investigations are the cornerstones of his romantic suspense fiction. Discover more on popular social networks and Wikipedia.

Visit the Author Profile page at Harlequin.com.

CAST OF CHARACTERS

Scott Lynley—An FBI special agent who reopens a cold case and solicits the victim's niece to help solve the case. Opening up a can of worms places the Chinese American beauty in danger and steels his resolve to protect as they grow closer.

Abby Zhang—An FBI victim specialist whose aunt, Veronica Liu, was murdered twenty years ago. Having discovered the body and still haunted by the unsolved crime, Abby is eager to work with the handsome cold case investigator in getting answers and opening her heart again.

Freda Myerson—The mayor of Kolton Lake who knew the victim and offers assistance in solving the case. But is she hiding something that could hinder the investigation?

Zach Gilliard—A mass shooting survivor who becomes fixated on Abby. But could his interest put her in peril and be linked to the cold case?

Selena Nunez—The detective who originally investigated the homicide and would like nothing better than to see the killer brought to justice.

Jeanne Singletary—Veronica's real estate business partner, who benefited professionally from her death, putting her under suspicion.

Oliver Dillman—A real estate agent who was once rejected by the victim. Did he seek payback through murder?

Prologue

Veronica Liu felt she was in a good place in her life. Her successful career as a real estate agent in Breckinridge County, Kentucky, was thriving. She had a great two-story residence right on the water in the town of Kolton Lake that she'd worked hard to be able to comfortably afford. Her up-and-down love life finally seemed to be going somewhere again, after being happily divorced for two years from a controlling man in Evan Liu. And perhaps most of all, she was delighted to be caring for her precocious but lovable twelve-year-old niece, Abby, whose Chinese American parents, Roslyn and Donald Zhang, died in a train accident when Abby was only six years old. Though she had no children of her own, Veronica considered Abby her daughter and planned to make it the real thing by formally adopting her.

Driving her white Mercedes-Benz AMG sedan down the yellowwood tree–lined Flagstone Lane that afternoon, Veronica pulled onto her property. She brought the car to a stop in the circular driveway. Her brown eyes gazed at the log cabin with loads of windows at every angle as she ran a hand through long black hair with blunt bangs. She knew this would all be Abby's someday. Or at least a place she could always come back to. In Veronica's mind, her late sister, Roslyn, would have done the same in caring for her daughter had their situations been reversed.

Veronica decided to make an apple pie, knowing it was Abby's favorite dessert. But first came dinner. Maybe leftovers to save time. When Veronica's cell phone rang, she lifted it from the pocket of her open-front blazer. She saw that it was an unidentified caller, who had disconnected. Wrong number? She was just about to get out of the car when she heard a noise. Turning toward the driver's-side window, Veronica saw the gun. It was aimed at her face. She had just enough time to meet the hard gaze of the familiar holder of the firearm before a shot went off.

It shattered the glass and struck Veronica point-blank. Everything went dark from that moment on. The instant death had deprived her of the opportunity to say goodbye to her niece. Or to identify her killer.

THE SHOOTER REACHED carefully through the shards of glass and checked the pulse of Veronica Liu in her neck, while ignoring her shattered face and splattered blood. When it became clear that she was dead, if not yet buried, the shooter took a moment or two to gloat, still holding the Colt Python .357 Magnum revolver before backing away from the vehicle as though it was about to explode. Giving the surroundings a sixty-degree look, there was no one in sight who would throw a crimp into the plan to escape the crime scene unscathed. Good. While there was no desire to kill anyone else, plans could always change if the situation warranted it.

When another glance indicated that the coast was clear, the shooter headed for the wooded area behind the victim's house and made for a clean getaway. The work was done and Veronica Liu would no longer be a problem. Certainly not one that couldn't be solved effectively, as had been the case.

The shooter got into a vehicle at a safe distance from the murder scene and drove off with no one the wiser and the target now a dead woman.

ABBY ZHANG WAS in the sixth grade at Kolton Lake Middle School. At twelve, six months away from turning thirteen, she was in the visual and performing arts club and on the problem-solving team. She wished her parents were still around to see her life today, but they weren't. But at least her aunt Veronica was there and always encouraging her to be the person she was meant to be. Abby took that to heart whenever she felt down, knowing her aunt was always looking out for her best interests.

When the school bus dropped Abby off about a block from her house, she waved goodbye to her friends and walked the rest of the way. Running a hand down her long black ponytail and holding her schoolbooks, she wondered what was for dinner tonight. Maybe they could go out for burgers and fries. As she neared the log cabin, Abby's big brown eyes took note of her aunt's car in the driveway. She was still inside the car, but didn't seem to be moving. Why?

Once Abby reached the vehicle, her heart raced when she saw the blood on her aunt's face. Or what was left of it. The girl screamed with shock, dropping the books. What happened? Who did this? Abby thought she caught a glimpse of someone disappearing into the woods. Even as she opened the car door and saw her aunt slump toward her, but otherwise showing no signs of life, Abby sensed what she dreaded to comprehend while wailing.

Her aunt Veronica Liu was dead.

Chapter One

FBI Special Agent Scott Lynley had a stack of case files spread across his L-shaped cherry desk. Specializing in cold case investigations, he'd been assigned to the Federal Bureau of Investigation's field office in Louisville, Kentucky. He hated the idea of homicides and missing persons under mysterious or suspicious circumstances going unsolved. Such as his last case. The decades-old strangulation death of Lexington resident Felicity Yamasaki lay dormant, with investigators unable to identify the suspect for years. Scott was able to discover a latent fingerprint and link it to a suspect, Blake Kitsch, who, when pressed, confessed to the murder in feeling a need to get it off his chest. The retired carpenter had been arrested and was now in the Fayette County Detention Center in Lexington.

At least the victim's surviving family was able to get some closure, Scott told himself, believing that was at least half the battle of his job. The other half was bringing the culprit to justice. He'd been at this with the Bureau for the last fifteen of his thirty-eight years of life, choosing to follow in the footsteps of his late parents, Taylor and Caroline Lynley, by having a career in criminal justice. His dad had been a chief of police with the Oklahoma City Police Department and his mom an Oklahoma County District Court criminal judge. After receiving his Bachelor of Arts in Criminal Justice from Southwestern Oklahoma State University, Scott had completed the new agent training session at the FBI Academy in Quantico, Virginia, and was off and running. His three younger siblings, Madison, Russell and adopted sister, Annette, had also found careers in law enforcement, with Russell becoming an FBI special agent too.

Scott had been divorced from his ex, Paula, for nearly a year now. He had hoped their marriage could have lasted as long as that of his parents, but it wasn't to be. Seemed as though the marriage couldn't survive the demands of their jobs and not spending enough time with each other. He hadn't dated anyone seriously since the divorce. Not that he was necessarily looking to get involved with someone. Or maybe he was, but the right person hadn't come along. Either way, for now he was content to concentrate on his work, jog for exercise in keeping his six-foot, two-inch frame in the best shape possible, or ride one of the horses on his ranch.

Stretching out a long arm, Scott haphazardly grabbed one of the folders and opened it to see the report on a twenty-year-old unsolved murder. Peering his gold-flecked gray eyes at it, he read about Veronica Liu, a thirty-one-year-old real estate agent who'd been shot and killed in her vehicle while parked in the driveway of her cabin in Kolton Lake, Kentucky, in Breckinridge County. A .38 Special cartridge case had been found at the scene. The round had been fired at point-blank range from a Colt Python .357 Magnum revolver that was never located. There was an unidentified DNA profile found inside Liu's vehicle, and a partial fingerprint detected on the outside of the car door, which may or may not have belonged to the perp, with no indication that this had been a robbery gone terribly bad.

A few suspects had been interviewed, but no arrests had been made and no clear motive established.

The victim had left behind a twelve-year-old niece, Abby Zhang, who'd reported seeing someone fleeing the scene, but had offered little to go on beyond that. Abby had been living with her aunt since she was six, when her parents, Roslyn and Donald Zhang, had died in a train derailment. *Talk about bad luck*, Scott told himself, no stranger to losing one's parents as his own had died in a car accident. But he'd been old enough at the time to be able to better process it.

With her aunt murdered, Abby Zhang had been sent to live with another relative. Scott wondered whatever became of the girl, who would be thirty-two today. Maybe he could talk with her. See if she could provide him with any useful information pertaining to the death of Veronica Liu. His thoughts were interrupted when Scott's superior, Diane Huggett, the assistant special agent in charge in the field office, entered his office. Tall, and in her midfifties, she had short blond hair with triangle layers, and was wearing one of her usual dark pantsuits and low heels.

Narrowing green eyes at him, she said, "Blake Kitsch killed himself."

Scott sat up in his well-worn, high-backed leather chair. "What?" He had been hoping to gather more information from the perp, including questioning him about a similar unsolved murder around the same time as the one Kitsch had confessed to.

"Looks like he was able to grab a pen from his attorney and stick it in his own neck, leading to a fatal outcome." Diane sighed. "The lawyer claimed that Kitsch admitted to killing another woman and just wanted this over and done with, before taking his action."

Scott scratched inside his thick short hair and asked interestedly, "Did Kitsch happen to name this other woman he says he killed?"

"It's still under investigation," she responded.

Scott frowned, fearful that Kitsch would take to the grave anything that might have closed another cold case. "At least Felicity Yamasaki can rest in peace that her killer was caught, no matter how long it took."

"Agreed." Diane glanced at his desk and the open folder. "What are you up to?"

"Looking into the murder twenty years ago of Veronica Liu," he answered matter-of-factly. "She was shot to death in her car, in the driveway of her cabin, and discovered that way by her twelve-year-old niece."

"Hmm…" The assistant special agent in charge was thoughtful. "Think you can solve this case?"

"I'd like to try." He had been given latitude to investigate cold cases that struck his fancy, only choosing to tackle those that left enough on the table to give him a fighting chance at cracking. More often than not, he'd been able to eventually solve them and help bring closure to the families and friends of the victims.

"Go for it." She gave her permission. "Every homicide needs accountability, no matter how long it takes."

"My sentiments exactly." He flashed a crooked grin.

"Whatever support we can spare will be available to assist you."

"Okay."

Diane smoothed a wrinkle in her linen jacket. "Keep me posted."

Scott nodded. "I will." He watched her walk out the door and then glanced again at the file on Veronica Liu. Who had killed her? And why? Might her niece, Abby, be able to give some clues? *I'd like to find out*, Scott told himself, as a good place to begin the investigation. He hoped she was cooperative, knowing that some secondary victims of violent crimes found it too painful to want to talk about. Even years later. Would that be the case here?

Opening up his laptop, Scott began an initial search for Abby Zhang, knowing that she could be anywhere or have a different surname now in marriage. There was also the possibility that she could be dead, for one reason or another. That last disturbing thought was put on hold when he spotted an article in the search engine, a few months old, about National Crime Victims' Rights Week, where an Abby Zhang was mentioned.

Clicking on it, Scott saw that the woman in question worked for the FBI as a victim specialist. Her job for the Bureau was to provide assistance and support for victims of crime. There was a photograph of her. Attractive and slender with long, dark hair and brown eyes, Abby Zhang looked to be in her early thirties, which would fit the age of Veronica Liu's niece today. The article indicated her deep commitment to aiding victims of crimes of violence.

That has to be her. Scott was amazed that the key witness to Veronica Liu's murder was actually an FBI employee. It certainly fit and was apropos, all things considered. With that in mind, he accessed the Bureau's site and confirmed that Abby Zhang was still employed as a victim specialist and working out of the Louisville field office's Owensboro resident agency.

Let's pay Ms. Zhang a visit, Scott mused after learning that she would be participating in an FBI human trafficking operation in Breckinridge County to rescue child victims and bring the traffickers to justice. He opened the top drawer of his desk, removed his Bureau-issued Glock 17 Gen5 MOS pistol from his leather shoulder holster and put it inside for safekeeping. He rose to his feet, wearing black loafers, and headed out for the two-hour drive.

NOT A DAY went by when FBI Victim Specialist Abby Zhang didn't think about the haunting loss of her aunt Veronica twenty years ago. The fact that her murder had gone unsolved was just as saddening to Abby. Seemed as though her aunt had simply become another statistic, buried beneath the piles of other homicide victims lost in the criminal justice system. Still, she had to believe that someday her aunt's killer would be identified and made to pay for taking a life Abby had been so dependent upon following the accidental death of her own parents.

Abby had been forced to go live with a distant relative, Kristin Shao, in the San Francisco Bay Area. Though it hadn't been an unpleasant experience, Abby had felt she was more of a burden due to obligation than a welcome addition to the family. It was only after she'd graduated from high school and went on to college that Abby realized her calling in life. She wanted to help other kids navigate through the difficulties all around during childhood tragedies.

Ten years ago, she'd followed up her Bachelor of Arts in Social Work with a Master of

Social Work from the University of Kentucky in Lexington, before taking a job with the FBI's Victim Assistance Program. Her specialty was child welfare after being primary or secondary victims of violent crime and/or sexual exploitation, but she was just as committed to making the transition from victim to survivor for all age groups.

Abby worked at the Bureau's satellite office in Owensboro, Kentucky, whose jurisdiction included Breckinridge County and Kolton Lake, where she'd spent part of her childhood and currently lived. At thirty-two, she was still single, having never found her soulmate and unwilling to settle for less. Why should she? Especially when she knew of others who had settled and were unhappy as a result. Till the right person came along, Abby was content with her work, along with favorite pastimes of jogging, swimming, and reading contemporary and historical novels.

Agents from the FBI's Crimes Against Children and Human Trafficking Program were currently in the midst of a human trafficking sting in Breckinridge County, with assistance from the Breckinridge County Sheriff's Office, Louisville Metro Police Department's Crimes Against Children Unit, and the Department of Homeland Security's Center for Countering

Human Trafficking. Abby was told that there were at least ten children believed to have been forced into prostitution and held captive by sexual exploiters and traffickers at a ranch home in an unincorporated community on Feldon Street.

Wearing an FBI jacket that seemed oversize on her slim body, Abby stood at a safe distance from the action, alongside Victim Services Coordinator Elise Martinez. She was a few years older, but looked younger with a cute two-tone pixie cut and curtain bangs, and blue eyes behind aviator-style glasses.

"How many of those poor children will need therapy for the rest of their lives?" Elise asked, wrinkling her small nose.

"Probably all of them," Abby answered truthfully, imagining what they had been put through by the pimps and johns. *No child should ever be sexually exploited or otherwise victimized by these creeps*, she thought. "But that doesn't mean they can't come out on the other side," she insisted, tucking an errant strand of curly sable hair behind her ear.

"I know. But still, it's hard." Elise had been the victim of sex trafficking and Abby felt for her, fully understanding her commitment to helping other victims.

"That's what we're here for, right?" she reminded the victim services coordinator. "To do whatever's needed to help them cope."

"Yeah." Elise pushed her glasses up. "Looks like it's about to go down. Let's hope everything goes according to plan."

Abby knew that the plan included an under-cover agent giving the go-ahead to agents and other law enforcement to storm the house while minimizing any further trauma to the victims. "It will," she responded more confidently than she truly felt. Even a slight wrinkle in the operation could prove costly for those who needed to be rescued. *And that would be disastrous*, she told herself.

As the team closed in, armed with Glocks and Colt M4 carbines, they burst into the home and shots were fired. Abby held her breath till she saw the children being led out by the authorities. All were disheveled and clearly traumatized, but alive. They were turned over to Abby and Elise, as the traffickers were rounded up, handcuffed and placed under arrest, while facing multiple charges related to the imprisonment, prostituting and sexual exploitation of minors.

After initial checks for obvious health issues, questioning, and provision of food and water, the victims were handed over to EMS workers for further medical evaluation and treatment.

Families were notified, or arrangements otherwise made for a safe environment to place the trafficking victims.

Abby felt a sense of relief that the children had been safely rescued, even with a long road of recovery ahead of them. *I'll do everything in my power to help them get through this*, she mused.

After conferring briefly with Elise and law enforcement on the scene, Abby was about to head to her car when she was approached by a tall, solidly built, handsome man who screamed FBI agent, judging by the air of confidence he exuded. She guessed he was in his mid to late thirties. His gray eyes were intriguing on an oblong, smooth-shaven face with a long chin. Thick black hair was styled in a comb-over pomp, low fade cut with an edge up. He was wearing a maroon polo shirt, navy chino deck pants and black loafers.

"Are you Abby Zhang?" he asked in a deep but pleasant tone.

"Yes," Abby confirmed while sensing he already knew that. "Who are you?"

"FBI Special Agent Scott Lynley, Louisville field office." He flashed his identification to prove it.

"How can I help you, Agent Lynley?" Abby wondered if it pertained to the current or a previous investigation she had participated in as a victim specialist. She was used to follow-ups from the FBI on the victims, often in relation to the ongoing cases against the perpetrators. Was that what this was about?

"I'm a cold case investigator," he said, and seemed to give her a moment to process that. "I've reopened the case into the death of Veronica Liu."

Abby reacted to this unexpected news. "You... you have?" she stammered, almost at a loss for words.

"Yes," he said. "If I'm not mistaken, Ms. Liu was your aunt?"

When she caught her breath, Abby felt herself traveling back in time to twelve years of age when her life was so different until that one fateful afternoon. She looked him squarely in the eye and said straightforwardly, "You're definitely not mistaken, Agent Lynley."

He grinned crookedly. "In that case, we need to talk, Ms. Zhang."

All things considered—and there were many when it came to trying to comprehend why her aunt Veronica had had to die, with the authorities seemingly looking the other way for answers, and why the FBI had chosen to restart the investigation after all these years—Abby couldn't agree more.

Chapter Two

Scott couldn't help but be impressed by Abby Zhang. To say that the online photo didn't do her justice would be a gross understatement. He loved her complexion on a gorgeous oval-shaped face, with enchanting bold cappuccino eyes, upturned nose, Cupid's-bow mouth and a cute, dimpled chin. Her long raven hair had layered bangs and was pulled back in a wavy chignon. He put her height at about five feet six inches, with a slender frame. Inside an FBI jacket, she was wearing a white ribbed top, blue straight-leg pants and beige moc toe loafer flats.

"Can I buy you lunch?" he asked her, believing it would make for a more comfortable setting to talk than outside or in an office.

Abby gave him a curious smile. "Sure, why not?"

"Good." He flashed a grin back. "Pick any place you like to eat at."

"Okay. There's a casual restaurant two blocks away that I go to often."

"Great. We can take my car."

She nodded. "Lead the way."

A couple of minutes later, they were riding in Scott's official vehicle, a black Ford Explorer SUV.

"So, looks like the sex trafficking operation went off without a hitch," he commented.

"Thank goodness," Abby said. "Had things gone south and any of the children been caught in the crossfire..." She paused. "Anyway, they were put through enough by the traffickers."

"I agree." Scott glanced over at her in the passenger seat. He could see just how seriously she took her job. Not that he could blame her for wanting to protect children, given Abby's own childhood ordeal where there had been no one present to prevent her from having to face it head-on. "The victimizers will pay the price," he promised her. "People like them usually don't fare very well behind bars."

"So they say." Abby faced him thoughtfully. "What led you to taking a look at Aunt Veronica's murder after so many years?"

It was a good question and one Scott usually got from family members of cold case victims, often in disbelief that their loved ones had not been forgotten. He took his eyes off the road for a moment to glance at his good-looking passenger and responded candidly.

"I get a lot of cold cases passed my way, including those that would not normally be federal cases in and of themselves but found their way into our sphere at the request of local law enforcement seeking assistance. In spite of their best efforts at solving at the time of the crime, some investigators run into a brick wall and the cases are pushed to the back burners. As a cold case investigator, that's where I come in. Some of these are more difficult than others to believe I might be able to crack. In this instance, the nature of the crime and manner of your aunt's death made me feel it was worth a shot." He paused. "What drew me to want to take on the case, in particular, was you."

"Me?" Abby fluttered her curly lashes. "I don't follow."

"You were twelve years old when Veronica Liu was murdered," Scott told her. "Losing the closest thing you had to a parent in such a violent way, at that point in your life, had to be devastating."

"It was," she uttered painfully.

"Not knowing why it happened and why the killer was never apprehended, I felt you deserved answers. Or, at least, I wanted to give it my best shot to make that happen."

"Thank you." Abby's voice broke. "Honestly, it's never sat well with me, the mystery of my aunt's death. I know the police had theories at the time and tried to piece them together and identify her killer. But as the years passed and nothing happened, I'd pretty much decided it was just something I'd have to live with."

"Maybe not," Scott indicated, knowing that he could only be prolonging her frustration with more disappointing results. Or lack thereof. But it was certainly worth pursuing for both of them, and he intended to do just that. With her help.

He pulled into the parking lot of Gwen's Grill on Bogue Road. They went inside and got a table near the window.

After ordering the soup of the day and a Reuben sandwich, to go with black coffee, Scott decided to ease his way into talking about Veronica Liu's death, and what Abby could remember about it, by getting to know a bit more about Abby herself. "How long have you been a victim specialist with the Bureau?" he asked.

Abby, who'd ordered iced tea, a veggie burger and fresh fruit, replied, "Nearly a decade now."

"That's a good while. You obviously like what you're doing." Scott considered her work indispensable to FBI operations in dealing with crime victims and their needs in the aftermath of victimization.

"I love being able to provide assistance to

those most in need during times of crisis," she acknowledged. "After being put through the ringer, without a lifeline from someone who cares, many victims would be totally lost. Especially child victims."

"I hear you and couldn't agree more. The Bureau's victim-centered method to investigations is what makes it so successful, and you're obviously a big part of that in your work with victims." He sipped the hot coffee and found himself wondering about her personal life. Or, more specifically, her love life. She apparently wasn't married, as near as he was able to determine. That didn't mean she wasn't happily involved with someone. Unlike him.

"What about you?" Abby got his attention. "How long have you been an FBI agent?"

"Fifteen years and counting," Scott answered proudly. "I come from a law and law enforcement family, starting with my parents and including a younger brother, also with the Bureau." Was that more information than she wanted or needed to hear?

"Interesting." As Abby tasted the iced tea, she seemed to mean it by the tone of her voice. "Have you always worked cold cases?"

"For about the last decade," he told her, having started out in counterintelligence and moving into investigating white-collar crime before voluntarily being assigned to his current duties. "I felt it was important to try and give a voice to those who no longer had one. Cold case investigations gave me that opportunity."

Abby smiled softly. "I'm glad you zeroed in on my aunt Veronica's murder," she said. "I can't begin to express how grateful I'd be if her killer could somehow still be brought to justice."

It was something Scott had heard many times before from family members of murder victims. Only, in this instance, it seemed to hit him in a more profound way, coming from Veronica Liu's niece. This put even more pressure on him to try to make things right for her. But could he? Or would this cold case remain on ice, despite his best efforts?

AFTER THE FOOD ARRIVED, Abby braced herself for needing to relive that awful day twenty years ago when she'd discovered her aunt's body. But painful as it was, she would gladly go through it if this could somehow result in the good-looking FBI agent being successful in his attempt to close the cold case.

She picked up her veggie burger and, before taking a bite, said contemplatively, "I'll tell you everything I can remember about my aunt Veronica's death, Agent Lynley."

He spooned his minestrone soup and said equably, "First of all, call me Scott. We're both on the same team here, so no need for formal titles."

"Okay, Scott." She grinned. "Abby is always preferred to Ms. Zhang."

"Good." His own grin was slightly crooked. "So, if you can go back to the day your aunt died, you reported to the police seeing someone in the woods behind the cabin. Is that right?"

"Yes." She moved her fork around the fresh fruit in a bowl. "At least, I believe so." Abby took a breath. "I was mostly focused on Aunt Veronica, as I could see that she was in a bad way. But when I looked up, it seemed as though someone or something was moving rapidly through the woods. Honestly, it could have been an animal. I can't say for sure, one way or the other. Everything happened so fast. After checking on my aunt, by the time I looked again toward the woods, I saw nothing. Sorry."

"Don't be." Scott spoke in a gentle voice. "You were understandably in a state of shock at the time and your primary focus would have been on your aunt." He paused. "You came upon the crime scene when you got home from school in the afternoon, right?"

"Yes."

"And it was still daytime?"

"Yes," Abby answered, forking a slice of pineapple.

"How far would you say you were standing in the driveway from where this person or animal in the woods was moving?"

Abby had never been particularly good at measuring distances. Still, she was willing to hazard a guess. "Maybe fifty yards," she speculated. "Or less."

Scott seemed to calculate this in his head. "That's a hundred and fifty feet. Close enough during the day hours to differentiate between an animal and human, don't you think?"

"Yes," she agreed, under normal circumstances. But that wasn't the case. "Except that the woods behind the property were a bit dense and I only caught a glimpse by happenstance, without truly homing in on it," Abby defended herself, even if knowing he was only trying to do his job. "Not to mention, I was too overwrought with emotion to think about anything but my aunt's terrible condition."

"Fair enough." He took a bite out of his Reuben sandwich. "You just never mentioned the possibility that you could have seen an animal."

"My first instinct then…even second and third, for that matter," she pointed out candidly, "was that it was a human being. I only mentioned the animal as a possibility in retrospect, given the craziness of the moment at hand." Abby ate more fruit. "Can't say if the person was male or female, as they were too far away and moving too quickly. I wish I could be more forthcoming."

"You're doing fine," Scott offered her reassurance. He sipped his coffee. "Did you see anyone else on foot or in a vehicle once you were off the school bus?"

"Not that I can recall," she responded. "The cabin was kind of secluded, so I would have noticed had anyone or a car caught my eye."

"When you went inside the cabin, was there anything that seemed off? Like someone might have been lying in wait for your aunt to get home?" Before Abby could respond, Scott added, "I know in the police report there was no indication of a break-in or anything that was reported missing. But maybe you can remember something that you didn't then?"

Abby sat back on the wooden seat, straining her memory for anything unusual inside the cabin. Nothing clicked. "Everything seemed normal inside the cabin," she told him. "The door was even locked. I doubt that the killer went inside." She sighed. "It's much more likely that the person came from the woods…" *And left the same way*, she pondered plausibly.

"Makes sense," he agreed coolly.

Abby felt a chill when thinking that this was likely the shadowy figure she'd seen in the woods, fleeing after killing her aunt. If only she had come home a little sooner, she might have frightened the attacker off. Seen the person to report to the police. *Or become a victim myself*, Abby thought frighteningly.

Breaking her reverie, Scott asked, "Can you recall if your aunt mentioned anything about having enemies?"

Abby pursed her lips musingly. "This probably sounds cliché, but as I told the police back then, everyone seemed to like my aunt Veronica. She was the type of person others quickly warmed up to." Abby recognized that this obviously wasn't the case with her killer. But had the person been a stranger? Or someone her aunt had known?

"Sometimes having that kind of personality can work against you," the special agent surmised, "strange as that may sound."

"It doesn't sound strange," she told him. "I've come across such people in my line of work, ones who were friendly to a fault and attracted some crazies who wished them harm." Was that what had happened to her aunt?

Scott leaned forward. "Did you ever witness any altercations between your aunt and someone else?"

Abby had to think about it again. "Only my uncle Evan Liu," she said, running a finger around the rim of her glass. "Before they got divorced two years prior to Aunt Veronica's death, they argued a lot, seemingly about everything. And anything."

"Think he would've wanted to hurt her?" Scott asked bluntly.

"No. I certainly don't believe he killed her, if that's what you're asking." Abby drew a breath. "Even with their difficulties, I think Uncle Evan never stopped loving my aunt and would not have wanted to see her dead. Besides that, he was remarried when she was killed and had a strong alibi for the time in question." For Abby, talking about this was harder than she'd realized, but she knew it needed to be flushed out, if it could help in any way in the reopened investigation.

Scott angled his head and asked, "What do you remember about your aunt's love life?" He added, "The police report seemed to indicate that she was seeing one guy in particular at the time of her death."

Abby rested an arm on the table. "Aunt Veronica seemed to date a lot, as I recall, but didn't share much about the specifics of her love life with me. I didn't learn till after her death that she had apparently been serious about a man she was dating, Mathew Yang, who, unbeknownst to her, was married at the time." Abby furrowed her brow. "Up until that point, my impressions were that Aunt Veronica was happily single, playing the game of romance by her own rules. Guess somewhere along the way, those rules were broken."

"Maybe your aunt was merely trying to protect you in her own way—" Scott tossed the notion out there "—by keeping a romance under wraps until she felt it was the right time to divulge it. If there would be such a time, in light of what she would likely have learned about Yang."

"I suppose you're right." Abby wondered if his deception could have led to murder. The fact that it was a cold case suggested it wasn't so cut-and-dried. She gazed at Scott and found herself wondering about his love life. Was he married? A family man? He seemed like the type of person who would not necessarily be satisfied being single and alone. But what did she know? Especially when her attempts at romance had fallen flat. Maybe some people weren't meant to live happily ever after. Was he one of those too?

"That should be all for now," Scott told her evenly, finishing off his second cup of coffee.

"Okay." Abby deduced from his words that

he intended to speak with her again. She found herself looking forward to it, which surprised her somewhat, as she didn't know him. But that could change.

When Scott drove them back to her car, Abby said, "I'm not sure how much I can offer in your investigation, but I certainly want to see justice served in my aunt's murder, at long last. As such, if you feel I can help in any way, let me know."

He hit her with that appealingly crooked grin again. "Count on it."

I will, Abby mused enthusiastically. She got out of his vehicle and into her own car, a red Subaru Solterra, and headed back to the FBI satellite office in Owensboro on Frederica Street.

That afternoon, Abby received an update on the condition of the rescued children, all of whom she was told were going to recover fully from their physical trauma and would be receiving extensive counseling to deal with the mental fallout from the captivity and sexual exploitation they'd endured. It only reinforced to Abby the urgency for the Bureau and local law enforcement to go after the human and sex traffickers, pimps and johns, and others who preyed upon children for profit and pleasure.

Then there were still the other child victims of crimes who were traumatized, either through direct or indirect victimization, when violence struck, and in sore need of specialists like herself to give comfort and hope. Abby now had a whole new reason for such in her own life. With Scott Lynley reopening the investigation into her aunt Veronica's murder, the possibility that it might finally be solved was a bridge Abby would gladly walk over in his company.

Chapter Three

Abby parked in the driveway of the two-story log cabin she'd inherited on Flagstone Lane from her aunt Veronica. She had heeded the advice from her aunt's friend and fellow real estate agent, Jeanne Singletary, to hang on to the valuable lakefront property, bordered by black walnut and yellowwood trees, for when she was ready to take possession of it. She did just that, moving into the residence five years ago, just as her aunt would have wanted.

Going inside, Abby took a sweeping glance at the spacious cabin with its vaulted ceiling, pine interior walls and floor-to-ceiling windows, which overlooked Lake Kolton, and had plantation shutters. She had chosen to remodel three years ago, putting her own spin on the residence. This included rustic engineered hardwood flooring, a stone fireplace and an eat-in L-shaped peninsula kitchen with a breakfast bar. She had replaced her aunt's more contemporary furnishings with log and handcrafted furniture, while adding some perennial house-plants such as silver vine and pink anthurium. A security system had also been installed for peace of mind.

Abby went up the straight staircase to the second floor, where there were two bedrooms, similarly outfitted, with the primary bedroom including an en suite, walk-in closet, and deck that overlooked a wooded area and the lake. Gazing at the woods through the window, she couldn't help but think about the conversation with Scott Lynley and the notion that those woods had provided a perfect escape route for a killer twenty years ago. And she may have seen the culprit. Or not.

Putting those uncomfortable thoughts on hold for now, Abby freshened up and let her hair down, retying it in a high ponytail. She was soon out the door and on her way to meet up with a friend, Beverly Welch, for a drink at the Yantun Club on Evemoore Drive. The two had bonded a year ago, after Beverly's husband, Julius, had been shot to death in a drive-by shooting and Abby had helped get her through it as a victim specialist. Though gang-related, the shooter had apparently targeted the wrong person, making the crime all the more tragic.

When Abby arrived, she found Beverly already seated at the table, waving her over. She worked her way through several other tables and was then greeted by her friend, who stood. African American and in her early thirties, Beverly was taller and just as slender, with a blond Afro worn in Bantu knots, and big brown eyes.

"Hey, girl," Beverly said spiritedly, giving her a little hug.

"Hey." Abby hugged her back.

"I took the liberty of ordering us both a Grey Goose Oaks Lily."

"Cool." Abby smiled at her, approving of the vodka cocktail that she liked.

They sat down and Beverly eyed her and asked, "So, what's going on? You sounded tense over the phone when you said you wanted to get together."

Abby sipped the drink thoughtfully. "My aunt Veronica's case is being reopened by the FBI. Or, one cold case agent, in particular," she told her.

"Seriously?" Beverly licked her lips.

"That was my reaction." Abby chuckled. "It's true."

"How did this come about?"

"Special Agent Scott Lynley took an interest in the case," she explained. "Seems as though he was touched by a little twelve-year-old girl being left to deal with something much bigger than her, after witnessing such a horrific scene."

Beverly gazed at her. "You?"

Abby nodded. "Yep."

"Wow." She tasted her drink. "How does it make you feel, having to dredge up old, painful memories?"

Abby pondered the question while tasting the drink. "Honestly, there are mixed feelings," she told her. "I hate having to go back there, when I was my most vulnerable and felt so helpless. But knowing my aunt died the way she did, and having no resolution, I want to know why she was killed and who was responsible for her death."

"Understood. You deserve some answers. I hope that the special agent can deliver them."

"So do I." Abby had learned long ago not to get her hopes up too high, only to be disappointed. But Scott seemed genuinely committed to the cause. For that, she had to believe he would be able to uncover what had been buried for two long decades.

"If he's successful, maybe you could send him my way," Beverly quipped. "Still waiting for some resolution in Julius's death."

"It's still an ongoing investigation," Abby pointed out, as far as she was aware. And currently a police matter.

"I know. But they seem to be dragging their feet, with no end in sight."

Abby felt her pain, considering the length of time she'd been waiting for her aunt's murder to be solved. "You just have to be patient," she told her gingerly. "I'm sure Julius's killer will be brought to justice." Was she really? Or would the gang win out and get off scot-free?

Beverly eyed her with skepticism. "You truly think so?"

"Yes." She kept her voice steady. "Most killers are eventually held accountable for their actions. No matter how long it takes."

Beverly gave a nod and Abby was sure she knew there was a double meaning to her declaration. It had been far too many years since her aunt Veronica had been laid to rest. But deep down inside, Abby had never given up on the belief that her killer would be brought to the surface, wherever currently submerged in hiding. No reason to back away from that now. Especially now that she had an ally in Scott Lynley in that regard.

The conversation shifted toward Beverly's ten-year-old son, Julius Jr., whom Beverly was doing her best to be both mother and father to at an age where he most needed parental guidance. It made Abby think about having children of her own someday and the joy it would bring into her life. As well as the potential heart-break were she to lose a child prematurely. Or to leave a child behind as the secondary victim of violence, much as had been the case in her own life.

She chose to remain on the positive side of bringing a child into this world. Now she just needed to meet, bond and fall in love with that special person of a like mind as a potential father to the child. For some reason, Special Agent Scott Lynley popped into her head.

Abby colored at the private thought while aware that it was way too premature, if at all, to think of the nice-looking FBI agent in romantic terms. Much less the father of her child. Wasn't it? Right now, it was much more important to want him to find her aunt Veronica's killer, whether alive or dead. And go from there.

DURING THE DRIVE back to Louisville, Scott had to admit that Abby Zhang had crossed his mind more than once. She had held up well in his questioning and provided him with some added perspective on her tragedy to work with. Apart from wanting to give her closure in the murder of her aunt Veronica Liu, the victim specialist seemed like someone he would enjoy getting to know better. She had left the door open in this respect, making herself accessible should he ever need to talk more about her aunt. So, no harm in taking advantage of the possibilities that could potentially present themselves, if Abby were also available, like him. If not, he would certainly be able to respect that and leave her alone.

Scott reached his ranch on Dry Ridge Road in good time, parking in the brick paver driveway. He had been living on the ten-acre, fenced property since purchasing it a decade ago, before prices had started to skyrocket in the city. The two-story, four-bedroom, Prairie-style house had been built at the turn of the twentieth century. In spite of various renovations over the decades, it had retained its architectural bones, which had attracted Scott to the place, reminding him on a small scale of the ranch he'd grown up on. This one came with a four-stall barn, where he kept two American Cream Draft horses and one Thoroughbred for leisure riding on the property's rolling hills and trails, amid tall, swamp white oak and southern magnolia trees.

He moved through the landscaped walkway and onto the long porch, supported by square columns, and went inside the house. It had an open concept with a great room, formal dining room and chef's-style kitchen, vinyl plank flooring and big windows throughout for natural lighting. The furnishings were a mixture of modern and vintage. Though the place suited him, and was his comfort zone, it still lacked the warmth of companionship. He'd had it once and lost it. Maybe he could get it back someday with the right person. Maybe not.

Scott went into the kitchen and grabbed a bottle of beer out of the Sub-Zero refrigerator. He opened it, took a sip and set it on the marble countertop. Taking out his cell phone, he called his brother, Russell, for a video chat. Being a fellow special agent who worked out of the FBI Houston field office, where his wife, Rosamund, was a Homeland Security Investigations special agent, Scott considered himself closest to Russell, among his younger siblings, though four years his junior.

After accepting the chat request, Russell's square face appeared on the small screen. Like him, Russell had their father's steel-gray eyes and prominent features. His jet-black hair was styled in a high and tight cut. He grinned. "Hey."

"Hello, Russ." Scott smiled at him. "Did I catch you at a bad time?"

"No. I've got a few minutes."

"Okay. So, what are you working on?"

"Just the run-of-the-mill bank robbery," Russell responded with a frown. "Happened yesterday in broad daylight in downtown Houston. A male and female pair, wearing hoodies and dark clothing while wielding semiautomatic handguns, made off with a few hundred dollars for their trouble."

"Not exactly a windfall for spending the next two decades behind bars," Scott quipped. "Have they been caught?"

"Not yet, but it shouldn't be long before we have them in custody." Russell looked at him. "What's the latest with you?"

Scott summarized the cold case investigation into the murder of Veronica Liu twenty years ago. He finished with, "I'm hoping that her niece, Abby Zhang, now thirty-two, and the only witness after the fact to emerge, can help to solve this case."

"Hmm…" Russell pinched the bridge of his nose. "Sounds like there's not much to go on at this point."

"That's often the case in age-old investigations," Scott pointed out. "Which is usually what makes them cold cases. But there is some unidentified DNA and latent print evidence that will need to be looked at again in a new light that may lead somewhere. Along with any original suspects who were passed over."

"Well, if anyone can crack a two-decades-old murder, it's you, Scott," Russell said flatly.

He grinned. "Thanks for the vote of confidence, little brother."

"Hey, just telling it as I see it," Russell insisted.

"As always, I'll dig as deep as necessary and see where it goes," Scott told him, tasting the beer.

They spoke a little longer before the call ended. Scott finished off the beer, changed into riding clothes, Western boots and a Stetson wool cowboy hat, and headed out to the barn for a ride on his Thoroughbred, Sammie. After saddling up and giving the sometimes-ornery horse some needed exercise, Scott couldn't help but wonder if Abby rode. If not, he would be happy to give her lessons one day, should she choose to accept.

THE FOLLOWING MORNING, Scott was up and at it for another day on the job. He wondered if he could come up with a good enough reason for a follow-up meeting with Abby. But first things first. He needed to speak with Art Reilly, the original FBI agent who'd worked the Veronica Liu case in conjunction with the local police department, and see what he could learn. Today, Reilly was the supervisory senior resident agent, heading the Louisville field office's Bowling Green resident agency.

Scott took the drive to Wilkinson Trace and

went inside the field office, where he was greeted by Art Reilly, who was muscular and in his mid-fifties, bald-headed and blue-eyed, with a horse-shoe mustache.

They shook hands as Scott said, "Thanks for meeting with me."

"Not a problem. Happy to do whatever I can to help in your investigation, Agent Lynley."

Scott gave him an appreciative nod. "Great."

"Why don't we step into my office?" Reilly told him and led the way inside. "Have a seat."

Scott sat on a soft-sided chair across from a double pedestal desk, which Reilly sat at. "So, what can you tell me about the original investigation into Veronica Liu's death?" he asked the supervisory senior agent in cutting to the chase.

Reilly pondered this for a beat and answered, "Well, after your call, I took a trip down memory lane to reacquaint myself with the case. As I recall, Ms. Liu was found slumped over in her car in her own driveway. Based on her positioning, it appeared as though she was caught completely off guard by her assailant and unable to react before being gunned down. My guess is that the unsub ran off into the wooded area behind the log cabin and probably made an escape in a waiting car in the clearing."

Scott rubbed his jawline. "Any thoughts on a motive?"

"There were a few, actually. Apparently, Liu had an active social and dating life, and a frenetic professional life. So, we considered that it could have been an act of jealous rage or revenge on the one hand. And on the other, a desire to eliminate her from the equation in the highly competitive real estate market in which she worked. Then, there was still the possibility that it was an attempted robbery and the robber panicked and took off without taking anything, other than the victim's life." Reilly sat back in his leather chair, his brow creased. "Unfortunately, we weren't able to pin it down, whichever way in terms of a suspect, that we could make stick. From there, the case went cold."

Scott thought about Abby finding her aunt's body. "Is it your sense that the killer may have been lying in wait for Veronica to arrive home? Or may have even lured her there?"

"It does stand to reason that the killer may have been hiding while waiting for Liu to show up," Reilly said matter-of-factly. "She did receive a call from an unidentified person just before the estimated time of death," he noted. "Could have simply been a wrong number. Or it may have been to draw her attention, giving the killer a further advantage in catching Liu off guard. The Kolton Lake PD took the lead in the investigation. You might want to speak with them for more details on the case and where things stand."

"I'll do that," Scott told him, having already planned to make that his next stop.

"If I come up with anything else that may be useful, I'll let you know."

"Appreciate that."

After getting up and shaking hands with the supervisory senior agent, Scott showed himself out. He wondered just how difficult it would be to crack the twenty-year-old case. Or was the devil within the details waiting to be unraveled?

Chapter Four

Abby got her day started by paying a visit to Jeanne Singletary, her aunt Veronica's best friend and former business partner, whom Abby had stayed in contact with through the years. As someone who had taken her aunt's death nearly as hard as herself, Abby wanted to tell her in person about Scott reopening the investigation.

After pulling her car up into the lot of Singletary Realty, Abby went inside. She spotted Jeanne, who was now the owner, seated at a laminate corner desk in front of a curtain wall. She was talking on her cell phone. In her mid-fifties, she was of medium height and slender build. Her short ash-blond hair was in a stacked bob cut and her blue eyes were covered with horn-rimmed glasses.

Abby wondered if she should have called ahead of time, but Jeanne waved her over. By the time she got to the desk, her late aunt's colleague had ended her phone chat. "Hello there, stranger." Jeanne spoke in a bubbly tone as she stood up in her designer lilac pantsuit and pumps and gave Abby a hug.

"Hi, Jeanne," Abby said, offering her a slight smile. "Sorry for just dropping in on you."

"Don't be silly. You're always welcome." She peered at Abby. "Is everything okay?" she asked, as if sensing the opposite.

Abby met her eyes. "The FBI has reopened the investigation into Aunt Veronica's murder."

Jeanne reacted in a stunned manner. "Really?"

"Yeah. A cold case special agent, Scott Lynley, has taken the case. He seems to think he can finally solve her death."

"Hmm…" Jeanne batted her lashes. "It's been twenty years, Abby. People come and go. Evidence disappears, which was apparently already lacking in the original investigation."

"I know," Abby conceded. "But if there's any chance at all of finding out who did this—"

"I'd like some answers too," Jeanne told her and took Abby's hands. "Veronica was my best friend and we started this real estate agency together. She would have loved to see how it's evolved over time to get to where it is today. I just don't want to see you get your hopes up again, only to be disappointed if this FBI agent doesn't deliver results you can take to the bank."

Abby squeezed her hands, realizing her concerns were coming from a good place. "I'm not twelve anymore," she said frankly. "I'll get through this either way. In the meantime, I can only keep my fingers crossed that Scott— Agent Lynley can unravel the twenty-year-old mystery."

"Me too." Jeanne met her eyes warmly.

"I suspect that Agent Lynley will want to talk to you at some point," Abby warned her, all things considered.

"Not sure I can add any more to what I told the police back then, but of course I'll be happy to answer any questions the FBI agent has. Thanks for the heads-up."

Abby nodded. When Jeanne's phone rang, it was the perfect time to say their goodbyes, with Abby promising to get together for dinner sooner than later.

SHE HAD JUST gotten to her nondescript, windowless office, and was at her workstation doing follow-up on the children they'd rescued from traffickers, when Elise Martinez came in and said, "Look what was just delivered!"

Abby smiled. She knew that Elise was currently in a serious relationship with a handsome firefighter, so sending her a bouquet of red roses was not surprising. "They're beautiful," she remarked.

"I was thinking the same thing." Elise moved closer. "The roses are for you."

"Me?" Abby widened her eyes. "From who?"

"You tell me. There's no card." Elise handed the flowers to her. "Secret admirer, perhaps?"

"Not so sure about that." Abby smelled the roses while considering whom they may have come from. Scott was the first thought to enter her head. Maybe it was a show of appreciation that she had been cooperative in his cold case investigation, even if that was a given in her own way of thinking. But why would he need to keep her in suspense? She also pondered that someone she had assisted as a victim specialist might have felt it was an anonymous way to express gratitude. She set the flowers on her desk. "Guess I'll just have to wait and see. Or maybe be left forever wondering."

"Hope not." Elise chuckled. "What fun would that be?"

"Not very," Abby had to admit. But right now, there were more important things on her plate. They began to talk about their latest undertaking, for which Abby brought up the movement of the victims. "From what I've gathered, they were shuffled around from house to house in an effort to stay one step ahead of the authorities," she noted.

"Didn't do the traffickers much good," Elise said. "Once the undercover agent was able to infiltrate their ranks and let the Bureau in on what the offenders were up to, they moved in and made the arrests."

"Thank goodness for that," Abby said. "I'd hate to think what might have happened if the victims had been relocated again, perhaps to another state, as so many others have had to endure, while their predators go about their business, hidden in plain view."

"I know." Elise pushed her glasses up. "Unfortunately, it's a never-ending cycle of child sexual exploitation and human trafficking in this country and elsewhere. I should know." Her brow furrowed thoughtfully. "Anyway, all we can do is be there for those rescued and see to it that they receive the best care available and let the system work in holding the perpetrators accountable."

"You're right." Abby knew full well that Elise, a survivor of sexual exploitation, was as committed to her job, as the victim services coordinator for the entire region under the jurisdiction of the FBI's Louisville field office, as she was. When her cell phone rang, Abby grabbed it out of the pocket of her linen pants and saw that it was Scott Lynley calling. "I should probably get this," she told Elise, resisting a smile in her eagerness to speak with him.

"Okay." Elise glanced at the roses and back. "Better put those in some water when you get the chance."

"I will." Abby waited until she'd left the office—having chosen to keep the cold case investigation to herself in the workplace till there was more to go on—before answering. "Hello."

"I'm about to go talk to Detective Selena Nunez, the original investigator who worked the Veronica Liu case for the Kolton Lake PD," Scott said. "She is still with the department. If you're game and have the time, I was wondering if you'd like to be there. Maybe hearing what she has to say might trigger memories. Or at least give you some greater perspective on where things stood when the case stalled."

"Yes, I would like to be there when you speak with the detective," Abby was quick to say. She recalled being interviewed by the detective twenty years ago, but had not seen or spoken to her since.

"I was hoping you'd say that." His voice was smooth and persuasive.

She agreed to meet him at the Kolton Lake PD in two hours, which gave Abby just enough time to do some work and anticipate seeing the FBI agent again.

SCOTT HAD JUST arrived at the Kolton Lake Police Department on Scoggins Street when he spotted Abby drive up. Admittedly, he'd wanted to see her as much for himself as to give her the opportunity to ask Detective Nunez anything Abby had wanted to ask as a twelve-year-old but had been unable to articulate at the time. *I'll try to keep my attraction to the attractive victim specialist in check for now,* he told himself, suspecting that might be a tall task as some things in life simply couldn't be helped.

He got out of his SUV and met her halfway in the parking lot. "Hey."

"Hi." She tucked a tendril of hair behind her ear, which Scott suspected was a nervous habit. The last thing he wanted to do was make her uncomfortable around him.

"Shall we go in?" he asked politely.

"Yes," she said. "Hopefully Detective Nunez can shed some light on the case that might help you in the investigation."

"That's the plan." On the way inside the building, Scott mentioned briefly his conversation with Supervisory Senior Resident Agent Art Reilly, who'd been involved in the original investigation for the Bureau. "Reilly has made himself available for further communication, while directing me to the lead investigator in the case."

"Hmm… I remember Agent Reilly," Abby stated thoughtfully as they entered the PD. "He seemed to be all business."

Scott laughed. "Some things never change."

"By the way," she asked casually, "you didn't, by chance, send me some roses, did you?"

"Uh, I'm afraid not." He gave her an unintended strange look. "Someone sent you roses?" A twinge of jealousy hit Scott while wishing he had been the lucky guy, whoever it was.

"Never mind," Abby uttered hastily, coloring as she walked ahead of him.

What was that all about? Scott wondered. Perhaps she would fill him in sometime on the details.

They went up to the second floor, where Selena Nunez stood from her cubicle desk when she saw them approaching. "Agent Lynley," she surmised.

"Yes," Scott acknowledged as they neared her.

"I'm Detective Nunez," Selena said, extending a small hand to shake his.

He did so and sized up the good-looking Latina. Midforties, slender and about five-eight, she had hazel eyes and brown hair in a textured lob. "Nice to meet you, Detective." Scott glanced at Abby. "This is FBI Victim Specialist

Abby Zhang." He noted for effect, "Veronica Liu's niece."

"Abby?" Selena arched a brow. "You're all grown up now."

Abby smiled softly. "Hello, Detective Nunez," she told her. "It's been a long time."

"Yes, it has." The detective shook her hand. After an awkward pause, she proffered a vinyl guest chair for one and grabbed a second from another desk for the other.

Once they were seated, Scott wasted no time in seeing what he could gather from her. "What can you tell us about the original investigation, Detective?" he asked evenly.

"Well, for starters, as I'm sure you read in the report, we were notified that a woman appeared to have been shot dead in a vehicle outside her home. She was identified as thirty-one-year-old Veronica Liu." Selena shifted uncomfortably in her desk chair. "I was assigned the case and went through the normal procedures of securing the scene, collecting evidence, interviewing witnesses and the like." Her brow creased. "In spite of chasing leads that turned into dead ends and having DNA and partial print evidence, unfortunately we were unable to establish motive or identify the killer. The FBI was brought in to assist and they, too, drew blanks, and the case went cold." Selena eyed Abby. "I

wish I had been able to catch your aunt's killer.
It still bothers me that I couldn't solve the case.
I'm glad that Agent Lynley is reopening it to
try and give you some closure."

"So am I." Abby glanced at him and back.
"I'm sure you gave it your best shot, Detective
Nunez, and I, too, wish things had turned out
differently." She took a sharp breath. "I wish
Aunt Veronica hadn't been murdered, and I'm
sorry that I wasn't more helpful when you interviewed me."

"Don't be." Selena waved this off. "You were
just twelve years old. I actually thought you did
a good job in telling me everything you'd seen
and done, including having the wherewithal to
report the crime. Based on the estimated time
of death and likelihood that the killer missed
seeing you by perhaps mere minutes, it's a
blessing that you're here today, alive and well."

Abby nodded meekly. "I feel the same way."

So did Scott, as he hated to even think about
her having been taken out of the equation by her
aunt's killer, depriving him of the opportunity
to meet her and maybe solve the crime together.
"Tell me about the suspects," he prompted the
detective, having only had a cursory look at
them in the file.

"I reacquainted myself with them," Selena
said, and opened the folder on her desk. "There

were really four suspects who stood out from the rest as possible murderers. Evan Liu, the victim's ex-husband, was obviously someone we took a hard look at. With no clear indication it was a stranger or random homicide, one that was intimate in nature was our primary focus. In spite of a bitter divorce, Liu's alibi held up.

"Mathew Yang was a businessman and had been dating Veronica at the time of her death, but apparently failed to inform her that he was married to someone else," Selena said. "He, too, was ruled out as the killer, along with his wife, Loretta Yang. Same was true for Katlyn Johansson, a bartender and exotic dancer whom Veronica had nearly come to blows with at the Tygers Club on Third Street the night before. And Bennie Romero, a meth addict who was seen wandering around the nearby wooded area shortly before the murder occurred. Other suspects either checked out or were low on the list due to circumstances and probability of guilt."

"Were there any similar-type murders at the time?" Scott asked curiously as the notion of a serial killer crossed his mind.

"Yeah, a few," she acknowledged. "But none that we believed could be linked to this case. In most instances, in fact, we were able to solve the crime." She frowned. "Sometimes we come up short."

Scott conceded this much, owing his current job as a cold case investigator to that reality. Still, it was hard to see a case fall between the cracks, leaving unsubs free to roam and possibly kill again. Whether or not Veronica Liu's killer had other dead victims remained to be seen. "Were you ever able to come up with anything else on the murder weapon?"

"Unfortunately, no." Selena ran a hand through her hair. "The ballistic evidence was submitted to the NIBIN," she said, which was short for the Bureau of Alcohol, Tobacco, Firearms and Explosives' National Integrated Ballistic Information Network, "and we failed to get a hit. I'm guessing that the shooter got rid of the Colt Python .357 Magnum revolver used in the crime, where no one could ever find it."

"Do you still believe that someone was targeting my aunt?" Abby posed the question directly to her. "Or could Aunt Veronica's murder be about something entirely different?"

Selena took a moment to consider the question before answering. "I definitely still believe this was a targeted attack," she said straightforwardly. "For lack of a better way to put this, someone wanted your aunt dead and made it happen. Who and exactly why remains a question mark." Selena gazed at Scott. "I'm happy to make all our files and evidence available to you for your investigation into the murder."

"Appreciate that." He gave her a nod, knowing that any stone that remained unturned just might hold the key to breaking the case. "If you come up with anything else relevant to solving the crime, Detective Nunez…"

"I'll be sure to contact you, Agent Lynley," Selena assured him clearly. "In the meantime, you might want to talk with two of Veronica Liu's friends who may be able to remember something they couldn't twenty years ago. Jeanne Singletary was her business partner and is still active as a local Realtor. Another person in Veronica's then inner circle was Freda Myerson—"

Abby practically blurted out, "As in Freda Myerson, the mayor of Kolton Lake?"

"That's the one," the detective responded. "At the time, she was Freda Neville. I'm sure that Mayor Myerson will be happy to cooperate in the investigation into her friend's death."

"I'll definitely pay her a visit," Scott said, and could tell that Abby was just as eager to speak with the mayor, too, who she apparently was unaware had known her aunt.

When they left the police department, Abby confirmed this. "I don't remember Aunt Veronica knowing a Freda Neville," she admitted.

"But, then again, I didn't know all her friends. Or apparently foes."

"What about her business partner, Jeanne Singletary?" He assumed that Abby knew in more than a passing glance whom her aunt had worked with.

"Yes, I knew—know—Jeanne," she told him. "We've kept in touch over the years since Aunt Veronica died. I actually went to see Jeanne this morning, knowing she would want to know that the investigation was being reopened." Abby looked at him. "I hope that was all right?"

"Of course." Scott grinned at her in concurrence. "As your aunt's friend and partner, she deserved to be kept abreast of what's happening."

"Okay." Abby smiled back at him.

"Why don't we go see Mayor Myerson, if you have the time?"

"I'd like that," she said, leaving no doubt that they were on the same page.

SELENA NUNEZ WENT back to her desk after seeing the FBI agent and Abby Zhang out. She again leafed through the case file for the murder of Veronica Liu. Selena had only been twenty-five and a second-year homicide detective for the Kolton Lake PD when handed the disturbing case. She'd had no idea at the time that it would go unsolved for the next two decades. In that time frame, she had gotten married, had three children and solved more than her fair share of murders, while moving up the detective ranks with the Homicide Unit.

But all that said, it still haunted Selena that she had been unable to bring Veronica Liu's killer to justice. And, as such, had failed to bring peace to some degree to that little girl. Now, Abby was a grown woman and, not too surprisingly, a victim specialist. Selena imagined it was her way to pay homage to the aunt she had lost. With the FBI reopening the case, maybe it could finally be solved once and for all. Or maybe, as with her own investigation, the leads would dry up and the murder would remain unsolved and the unsub would remain unidentified.

Selena sucked in a deep breath. Her gut told her that Agent Scott Lynley just might succeed where she had failed. Or, at least, it seemed as though he was all in on helping Abby get over the hump. If so, this would certainly be welcome news to Selena as well. After all, a win would still be a win. No matter how long it took to achieve success.

Selena grabbed the cell phone off her desk and gave Mayor Myerson a courtesy call to let her know she was about to have company.

Chapter Five

Abby was still pondering the notion that her aunt Veronica had been friends with Mayor Freda Myerson. *How did I not know this?* she wondered as she accompanied Scott for the short drive to the mayor's office on Walton Road. Although she hadn't been privy to everyone in her aunt's life, Abby felt she'd at least had a handle on those her aunt had been most chummy with. Apparently not.

"Don't know if we can get anything useful out of the mayor." Scott broke into Abby's thoughts. "But it's worth a shot as I try to lay the groundwork for reinterviewing suspects who are alive and nearby, for starters."

"I couldn't agree more," she told him from the passenger seat of his vehicle, while not getting her hopes up. "If nothing else, it would be nice to speak with someone my aunt Veronica was acquainted with, for memories' sake."

"I hear you." His voice was reflective and

made Abby want to know more about his background. And, for that matter, the status of his own family life today. She was starting to sense that he wasn't married after all. Or was that wishful thinking on her part? "So, what's up with the roses?" he asked abruptly, glancing at her.

"Roses?" She pretended she was dumbfounded with the question.

"You mentioned earlier about receiving roses. Have any idea who they came from, once I was knocked out of the picture?"

"Not really." Abby cocked a brow at his bluntness. "They just showed up at my office this morning with no card." She felt silly assuming they'd been sent by him.

"Really?" Scott jutted his chin. "Maybe someone you are or were dating?"

"Haven't dated anyone in a while," she told him, "if you must know." Or was that his way of asking if she was single? "I suspect the roses may have come from someone I helped as a victim specialist, but didn't want to make a big deal out of it by identifying themselves."

"Okay." He left it at that, as though satisfied.

"So, what about you?" Abby decided that she may as well get her own curiosity over with. "Are you single, married, dating someone, what?"

"I'd say 'what' probably is the best answer." Scott gave her a crooked grin with a glint in his eye. "I'm divorced, single and unattached."

"I see." She found herself relieved in hearing this. Or was excited more appropriate? "Guess we have that much in common," she said lightly, even as she wondered how someone had managed to let him get away.

"Yep," he concurred, grinning. "Looks that way."

Neither of them spoke the rest of the way, but it certainly gave Abby food for thought as she wondered what to do with the information. If anything.

When they arrived at the office, she brushed shoulders with Scott, sending an unexpected wave of electricity through Abby. Had he felt it too? Or had she convinced herself of something that wasn't truly there, other than in her head?

They were shown into the mayor's spacious office and she was standing there to greet them. "Freda Myerson," she said coolly by way of introduction.

"Special Agent Scott Lynley."

"Abby Zhang." She studied the attractive woman who'd known her aunt Veronica. In her early fifties, Freda was several inches taller and not quite as slender as Abby, but seemed just as fit, wearing a designer navy skirt suit and low heels. Her curly dark hair was medium length and parted squarely in the middle. Abby tried to picture the twenty-years-younger version, but drew a blank for recognition.

Scott stuck out his hand. "Thanks for seeing us on short notice, Mayor."

"Not a problem," she contended. "Detective Nunez told me you were on your way and what this was all about. I have a few minutes before a meeting I have to attend." Freda turned big blue-green eyes onto Abby. "I can see the resemblance between you and Veronica," she expressed, taking her hands. "I'm sorry I never got the chance to formally meet you twenty years ago, Abby."

"Me too." She met Freda's steady gaze, and in so doing, Abby could almost envision her as someone in attendance at her aunt Veronica's funeral. Had she not been so overwrought with emotion at the time, Abby might have remembered her.

Freda released her hands, smiled warmly and said, "Why don't we sit down?" She eyed a small area by a window that included three fabric lounge chairs surrounding an oval conference table.

Once they were seated, Scott said equably to her, "I understand that you and Veronica Liu were close."

"I wouldn't exactly say that we were close," Freda corrected him in a level tone. "Veronica sold me my first home, and we went out a couple of times for drinks, and maybe met once or twice in relation to the purchase. But that was about it."

He sat back pensively. "Detective Nunez seemed to believe that you were part of Veronica's inner circle," he said. "You're saying this wasn't true?"

Freda took a calming breath. "Not sure how the detective drew that conclusion," she argued. "Yes, I was friendly with both Veronica and Jeanne Singletary, her real estate partner, after establishing a good working relationship with them as a home buyer. I wasn't part of Veronica's inner circle, though, or vice versa. When I heard about what happened to her, of course I was broken up by it, like everyone else who knew her. Especially since I was aware that she was leaving behind a little girl." She eyed Abby sorrowfully. "I gave a statement to the police to that effect, outlining the nature of my association with Veronica. Never had any follow-up after that." She paused. "I did attend the funeral to pay my respects to Veronica," she uttered, thoughtful. "It never occurred to me at the time that her murder would go unsolved all these years."

Abby choked up at the heartfelt words, considering she was of the same mind. Even if the mayor hadn't been very close to her aunt Veronica, the fact that they'd known each other at all was a connection of sorts between the past and present. "Mayor Myerson, in the time you spent with my aunt, did she ever mention anything about someone who may have wanted to harm her?" Abby asked keenly.

Freda looked her in the eye and replied without preface. "Veronica never told me someone was after her, if in fact this was personal, as opposed to an attempted robbery or random attack. In our conversations, your aunt seemed very likable and not one to get on someone's bad side. Obviously, that did happen, for whatever reason, and I'm happy to see that the case has been reopened. Veronica left us—and you, Abby—way too soon. You both deserve some resolution to this." Freda looked at Scott. "As mayor of Kolton Lake, if there's anything you need to help facilitate cooperation with the police department, please let me know."

"I will," he promised.

"Good." Freda stood, indicating the chat was over. "Well, I have a meeting to go to. I'll walk you out." At the front door, she shook both their hands and said, "I'm sure your aunt would have been proud, Abby, to see that you've grown up to become a lovely young woman."

Abby blushed. "Thank you."

"I agree," Scott pitched in. "Abby also happens to work for the Bureau as a victim specialist."

"Really?" Freda bobbed her head. "All the more impressive."

"It's a good fit for me," Abby said as though she needed to explain her choice of profession to someone who had succeeded in her own right as the mayor of Kolton Lake.

"I'm sure it is."

Freda's sympathetic expression seemed to acknowledge the fragile line between being a victim and survivor, which Abby now considered herself. Albeit now one on a new mission. Or at least with a new ray of hope. That was to finally get to the bottom of Aunt Veronica's murder, with the help of Scott Lynley.

SCOTT WAS GLAD to see that he had the cooperation of Mayor Freda Myerson, should she be needed to run interference with the Kolton Lake PD. He doubted it would come to that, as Selena Nunez seemed more than supportive in assisting in any way she could on the cold case she'd originally investigated. That included the detective turning over forensic evidence taken from the crime scene, which he planned to have retested at the FBI Laboratory in Quantico, Virginia, for a possible match with a known offender. It would be up to him to continue to do some digging and see what he could unearth in the investigation.

Though he enjoyed spending official time with Abby, Scott reluctantly drove her back to her vehicle in the police department's parking lot. Clearly, she was enthusiastic about playing a role in cracking the mystery of Veronica Liu's death. But she had her own work with the Bureau and he needed to respect that without overstepping for his cold case. On the other hand, there was no reason why they couldn't continue to see each other on a more personal level, if she were willing.

He turned to Abby, who seemed to be lost in thought, perhaps feeling a bit let down that Freda Myerson was not as close to Veronica as advertised. Consequently, she'd been unable to fill in any of the blanks that Abby may have been seeking in learning more about her aunt from the mayor. "Would you like to grab a bite to eat this evening, once we're both off the clock?" Scott asked her tentatively, hoping she was game.

Abby looked up at him and smiled. "Yes, that would be nice."

"Great." He grinned back, thoughtful in remembering the veggie burger she'd ordered for lunch at the restaurant. "So, are you a vegetarian?" he asked curiously, if only for the record.

"No," she surprised him by saying. "If you're referring to the veggie burger, I think it's healthier and tastier than regular burgers, but otherwise, I wouldn't say I dine on a vegetarian diet."

"Just checking." Scott looked at the steering wheel. "Would have been fine either way."

"Nice to know." After a beat, Abby suggested, "We could have dinner at my place. As it's the same cabin my aunt Veronica lived in twenty years ago, it would give you an opportunity to check out the surroundings for some perspective in the investigation into her death."

That made sense to Scott on multiple levels, not the least of which being that they would get to dine in a cozier setting than a restaurant. Then there was the fact that he hadn't realized Abby was living in the same location as the scene of the crime. He imagined that was both a difficult and a practical way to move on as a grown woman herself now. Last, perhaps the setting could provide some clues as to the crime and getaway, even after all these years.

"You're on," he told her. "But I'll bring the wine. Or whatever your pleasure."

"Wine sounds good," she said. "Red or white?"

"White wine, it is." Scott stopped in front of

her car and they set a time for six o'clock, giving him some leeway for more interviews. "See
you later," he said as Abby unbuckled her seat
belt and opened the SUV door.

"All right." She got out. "'Bye, Scott."

"'Bye." He waited until Abby was inside her
vehicle before driving off, already counting the
hours till they met again.

ABBY ADMITTEDLY FELT giddy at the prospect of
making dinner for Scott, while trying to decide
on the meal. They said that the key to a man's
heart was his stomach. She wasn't necessarily
seeking his heart at this point. After all, it could
have been closed off to newcomers—or at least
held back—following the collapse of his marriage. But she did relish the opportunity to get
to know the FBI agent on a more personal basis.
And vice versa. She started the car, backed out
of the slot, and drove out of the parking lot and
onto the street, just in time to see Scott's SUV
turn right on a main street. Abby imagined he
would be poring over any evidence available.
As well as speaking with anyone who had been
interviewed originally, including Jeanne Singletary, while trying to connect the dots as cold
case investigators needed to do if they were to
succeed in their mission.

Abby's thoughts turned to Freda Myerson.

In spite of wishing the mayor had given them more to go on as a confidante of her aunt Veronica's, that hadn't been the case. This meant the lingering questions would continue to linger longer as the investigation unfolded. And Abby had to be prepared to face the reality that she might never get a complete picture of her aunt. Or the circumstances that had led to her murder.

While barely realizing how she had gotten there, Abby found herself at Kolton Lake Cemetery. It was where her aunt Veronica was buried. The reopening of the investigation had given new life to the possibility that her death could finally be solved. Leaving her car, Abby felt compelled to visit the gravesite of the woman who'd been like a mother to her for six years of Abby's preteen life.

Walking across grass wet from sprinklers, she made her way to the spot where Veronica Liu had been laid to rest. Abby touched the granite headstone, as if touching the spirit of her aunt. "Miss you, Aunt Veronica," she said out loud. "Wish you could see and talk to me now."

Abby said a silent prayer and extended this to her parents as well. Just as she was about to leave, Abby heard the squishing of footsteps behind her. She turned around and saw a tall man standing there.

"Did you get the roses?" he asked succinctly.

It took Abby a moment as she studied the man who was in his early forties and long-limbed, with light brown hair in a spiky cut. He was staring back at her with dark, foreboding eyes. Abby recognized him as Zach Gilliard, a survivor of a mass shooting at a shopping center in Grayson County last month, before the gunman killed himself. Zach had suffered only minor injuries but had been traumatized nevertheless by the incident the FBI had investigated as part of a joint task force. Within her duties, Abby had provided crisis intervention for Zach and other victims of the crime.

"You sent them?" Abby asked him with uneasiness.

"Yeah," Zach acknowledged. "Hope you liked them."

She stiffened. It wasn't uncommon for victims, or near victims, of traumatic incidents to become fixated somewhat on victim specialists. Still, seeing Zach at the cemetery, of all places, was a little creepy. Had he followed her there?

"They were nice," she placated him. "But you really shouldn't have."

"I wanted to give them to you," he insisted. "It was the least I could do when you were there for me after I saw my life flash before my eyes."

Abby looked at him with alarm. "What are

you doing here?" She hadn't necessarily seen him as a dangerous person. Or a stalker. Could she have misjudged the man?

Zach raised his hands as if in mock surrender. "Don't be afraid," he said. "I'm not going to hurt you. I was at the police department to donate some items and saw you there. Before I could speak with you, you'd gotten in your car and driven off. I thought you might be headed back to your office, where I was going to make sure you received the roses as my way of thanking you for helping me out. I didn't leave a note because I didn't want you to get the wrong impression. Anyway, when I saw you go into the cemetery, I figured it was as good a place as any to say what I needed to. Sorry if I scared you."

"It's fine," Abby told him, remaining wary. "Again, thanks for the roses, but I was just doing my job." Didn't he get that?

"I know and I appreciate it." He glanced at the headstone. "A relative?"

"Yes." She left it at that, having no wish to elaborate on something that was none of his business.

Seeming to pick up on that and her uncomfortableness, Zach said, "Well, I'll let you get back to paying your respects. See ya."

I don't think so, Abby thought, not seeing any reason why she would need to follow up with him as a victim specialist. "Goodbye, Zach," she told him simply.

She watched him walk away till out of sight and then turned back to her aunt Veronica's grave, where she spoke a few more words of sympathy, remembrance and regrets, before leaving.

Still a bit rattled from the unexpected presence of Zach Gilliard, Abby hurried to her car and locked the door once safely inside. She saw no sign of the unemployed warehouse worker, breathing a sigh of relief.

After starting the car, Abby drove from the cemetery. She checked the rearview mirror to see if she was being followed. There was no indication of such. She remained tense, nevertheless, until getting back to the safety of the FBI's Owensboro resident agency.

Chapter Six

Scott parked in the lot of Singletary Realty for a visit with Veronica Liu's business partner, Jeanne Singletary. The fact that she had kept in touch with Abby through the years was a good thing. Even better would be her ability to provide clues as to who might have killed Veronica.

He walked inside the real estate office and saw a slender twentysomething male with brunette hair in a topknot fade on the phone at one desk. Angling his eyes, Scott faced the owner, recognizing her from the picture on the front window of the office. She was seated at her desk and, when spotting him, stood and approached with a smile on her face.

"May I help you?"

"Special Agent Lynley." Scott flashed his identification. "Jeanne Singletary?" he asked rhetorically.

"That would be me." She stuck out her hand

and shook his. "Agent Lynley. You want to talk to me about Veronica," she said knowingly. "Abby told me you would come by."

"I'm aware that she visited you," Scott said. "I'd like to go over a few things in your original statement to the police and see if you might have missed anything pertinent in the investigation."

"Of course." Jeanne pushed her glasses up. "I'm happy to cooperate in any way I can. Why don't we go over to my desk?"

Scott followed her to a corner of the office that was all her own. She sat back at her desk and he took a seat across from her in a swivel guest chair. Before he could question her, Jeanne said, "Honestly, I was surprised to learn that the FBI was taking another look at the case. How did this come about, if I may ask?"

"You may," he told her. "We typically try to keep even the coldest cases in our viewfinder, hoping the day will come when we can still crack the case. I took an interest in this one, given that the death of Veronica Liu totally upended the life of her twelve-year-old niece. I felt that even twenty years later, Abby deserved some answers."

"I agree. She should learn why someone killed her aunt. If that's possible so many years later." Jeanne lifted a brow musingly. "Has new evidence surfaced?"

"I'm not at liberty to say." Scott went with the standard line when questioning parties pertinent to a criminal investigation. Not to say that he considered Jeanne Singletary a suspect, per se. She had been cleared by the original investigators, but the fact remained that she'd stood to gain the most financially by Veronica's death. And it appeared as though she was still riding that wave as the owner of the real estate agency. "Why don't you tell me what you remember about that time in Ms. Liu's life?"

"All right." Jeanne squared her shoulders. "Veronica was a hard worker and was just as hard in her play. She loved the rewards of success as measured against the risks of failure. We didn't always see eye to eye on every aspect of running a business. Much less our romantic ups and downs, but we always had each other's backs. I was very sorry to lose my dear friend."

Sounded sincere enough to Scott, but good actors could be convincing, were that the case. "You told the police that you didn't know of anyone who would have wanted Veronica dead. Do you still stand by that?"

"Yes," Jeanne uttered. "I mean, professionally speaking, we worked in the cutthroat business of real estate so, theoretically, someone could have wanted one less competitor. But if that was the case, I should have been killed too." She took a breath. "Yet here I am, alive and well."

"You make a good point," he allowed, if not one that hadn't already been accepted for years by investigators. This didn't mean it was rock-solid, though, with a fresh set of eyes. "What can you tell me about Ms. Liu's romantic life?"

"Veronica was ever the optimist when it came to romance," she indicated. "Problem was she never seemed to get it right when it came to picking men. But not for lack of trying. First there was her ex, Evan Liu, who barely gave Veronica room to breathe. She finally kicked him to the curb, but didn't have much better luck with the other men who came along. That included her last boyfriend, Mathew Yang. She thought he might be the one. Except for the fact that he was married to someone else."

"Did Veronica know about the wife?" Scott stared across the desk while wondering if Yang's wife had known about his having an affair and with whom.

"Not to my knowledge." Jeanne leaned to one side in her faux leather ergonomic chair. "I think that Veronica was even planning to spend a week with him in Hawaii, and maybe take Abby with them."

But that never came to pass, Scott told himself. Someone saw to that. He moved on. "Was there anyone you can recall that Ms. Liu had a problem with for whatever reason?"

Jeanne pondered this and responded, "As I told the police back then, one of our agents, Oliver Dillman, did hit on Veronica. She made it pretty clear that she wasn't interested."

"And how did he take it?"

"At first, he didn't seem to want to take no for an answer," she claimed. "But, eventually, he got the message." Jeanne frowned. "Unfortunately, after Veronica's death, Oliver tried to put the moves on another female agent. Enough was enough. I fired him."

Scott vaguely remembered seeing Dillman's name in the cold case file as a suspect who hadn't made the main suspects category. Maybe he merited a second look. "Do you know where Oliver is today?"

"As a matter of fact, I do." Her voice dropped an octave. "He's now an agent at Murlock Realty Group, a competing real estate office in Kolton Lake."

Scott made a note. "That should do it for now." He stood. "I won't take up any more of your time."

Veronica remained seated. "I hope for Abby's sake that you find what—or who—you're looking for, Agent Lynley."

"Thanks." He gave her a crooked smile. As another passing thought entered his head, Scott asked curiously, "I understand that you and Veronica were friends with Mayor Freda Myerson?"

Jeanne nodded musingly. "Yes, we knew Freda long before she became mayor, after selling her a nice town house. We weren't close or anything, but I do remember that she gave a fun housewarming party. After Veronica died, we lost touch."

"At least you can say you knew the mayor way back when," he said in a lighthearted manner.

"True." She gazed up at him. "I prefer not to live in the past though. Except, of course, for the fond memories I'll always have of Veronica."

He accepted that at face value. "I'm sure Abby feels the same."

ABBY HAD TOSSED back and forth whether to go with Char siu, which was a Chinese-style roasted pork, or baked chicken and mushrooms, as the main home-cooked dish. She decided on the former, having learned it from her aunt Veronica, along with peas, honey-glazed carrots and cornbread muffins. A homemade apple pie, her favorite dessert, would complete the meal. She hoped it would meet with Scott's approval, after being used to cooking only for herself in recent memory. At least it would give them an opportunity to see if the sparks she felt were there between them were real or not. She certainly wasn't getting her hopes up too much, having been there and done that with less than ideal results. Would this be any different? Or should it be, since their primary focus was on solving her aunt's murder? So why couldn't both be a possibility?

Abby calmed her nerves as she tended to the food and, when ready, left the kitchen to change clothes and wash her face. She wore little makeup and saw no reason to change that. Her hair was let loose and she brushed it across her shoulders. When she heard a car drive up, Abby peeked out the window and saw that it was Scott. She felt a tingle at the thought of kissing him, but allowed it to subside as she went outside to greet him.

Abby smiled as she watched him get out of the car. "Hey."

"Hey." Scott grinned and held out the bottle of white wine. "For you."

She took it from him. "Thanks."

He glanced about and commented soberly, "So, this is where it happened?"

"Yes." She had a feeling that he had looked at crime scene photos to correspond with the precise location. "Aunt Veronica was murdered precisely where you're standing."

He stepped away, as if it was hallowed ground. "Sorry."

"It's okay. That was twenty years ago," she reminded him. "So it's not nearly as unsettling to step or drive on the spot today." Never mind that the memories couldn't help but resurface by the very nature of his investigation.

"I suppose it wouldn't be." Scott gazed at the wooded area that Abby knew had filled out even more over the years. "The unsub had to have been familiar with this location and the best way to commit the crime and escape without merely getting into a car that could be seen and described by witnesses, along with the driver. Or anyone else inside the vehicle."

"I agree," Abby said, wondering if there could have been more than one person involved in the crime. And if her aunt had actually been targeted for reasons still unknown.

"Why don't you show me around inside?" Scott told her. "Then we can eat, whenever you're ready."

"Okay." She led him into the log cabin, wanting Scott to have a feel for the place that might somehow play on his mindset in trying to reconstruct the cold-blooded murder of her aunt Veronica and how the cold case might start to warm up.

SCOTT HADN'T NEEDED long to size up the landscape surrounding Abby's property. There was the lake on one side and the wooded area on another. He didn't imagine Veronica Liu's killer making his or her escape by boat, though not impossible. No, the greater likelihood was that the trees formed the perfect cover for a getaway. Whereas the street was the worst means for leaving the scene of a murder. Given the case had aged by two decades, with no killer in custody, that would seem to rule the possibility out.

While taking in the scent of food in the air and before touring the place, Scott turned his attention to the woman of the house. Abby was wearing a white V-necked top, gold Bermuda shorts, showing off shapely legs, and flats. He wondered if she knew how sexy she looked, enhanced by wearing her long hair down.

"Nice place," he told her at a glance, though knowing it came at a high price, after what she had lost.

"Thanks." Abby gave him a thoughtful look. "My aunt Veronica left it to me. It took me a long time to lay claim to it, but I decided she wouldn't have wanted me to sell simply as a means to block out what happened. For one, I couldn't even if I tried. Then there's the fact that I happen to love this location by the lake and wouldn't want to give it up for the wrong reason."

"I understand." Scott wondered if the right reason to sell would be if something—or someone—better came along that might make her rethink her position.

"I'll give you the grand tour before we eat," she told him.

"All right."

Scott followed her as Abby walked him around downstairs and then upstairs. He couldn't help but be impressed with the original architecture of the cabin, as well as the remodeling. At the same time, he found himself imagining Veronica Liu living there with the young Abby before everything had changed irrevocably for both of them. Someone out there needed to be held accountable for that.

Peeking inside the primary bedroom, Scott couldn't help but home in on the hickory log bed and pictured himself on it with Abby, cuddling and the rest. That flicker of desire inflated as she inadvertently touched him while moving on down the hall before lessening as they headed back downstairs.

He helped bring the food and drinks to the rustic reclaimed-wood dining table, then they sat across from one another in pine log chairs and began to eat.

"It's delicious," Scott said of the Char siu, which Abby had revealed had been passed on to her from her aunt.

Abby smiled. "Glad you like it."

I like you even more, he mused, imagining that this was something he could get used to. "I'm always up for new dishes," Scott said. "And old ones too."

"Good." She scooped up some peas, put them in her mouth and, after eating, said, "So, I had a rather odd encounter after we parted at the police station."

"Oh…?" He met her eyes. "Tell me about it."

"I went to visit Aunt Veronica's gravesite and a man showed up there without warning." She paused. "His name is Zach Gilliard. He survived the mass shooting last month in Grayson County."

"Yeah, it was a terrible incident," Scott acknowledged, frowning.

"Anyway, though Zach wasn't seriously hurt, he was understandably pretty shaken up by what happened. As a victim specialist, I was there to offer him and others support. Nothing more. Then, yesterday, I received those roses anonymously."

"They were from him?" Scott asked, wide-eyed while forking honey-glazed carrots.

"Yes." Abby tasted her wine. "He followed me to the cemetery from the police department, where Zach claimed he was only there to donate some items, and just wanted to acknowledge sending the flowers and thank me again for assisting him."

"You think he was stalking you?"

"I don't know," she admitted. "Maybe it was a harmless one-off. In my line of work, you do get some victims or near victims developing a fixation that is usually short-lived. Hopefully, that's the case here. If it was even that."

"It's easy enough to check out his story about donating goods to the Kolton Lake PD," Scott pointed out, and tasted the wine.

"I suppose."

"Of course, even if true, it could still have been a pretext for stalking." He had come across dangerous stalkers as an FBI agent and Scott knew they could never be taken lightly. Including those whose behavior could escalate from little more than a nuisance to deadly. "I'll give the police department a call," he told her. "And also do a criminal background check on Zach Gilliard, to be on the safe side."

Abby nodded. "Thank you."

"No problem." On the contrary, Scott didn't want to see any harm come to her from a stalker or anyone else. "If Gilliard threatens you in any way, let me know."

"I will." They ate in silence before she asked him, after biting into a cornbread muffin, "So, I take it you live in Louisville?"

"That's correct." He grinned. "I have a ten-acre ranch with a few horses."

"Seriously?" Her eyes widened with fascination. "How cool."

Scott laughed. "Well, this is the Bluegrass State." That, in his mind, went hand in hand with cowboys, pastures, horses and the like.

"True." She chuckled and sipped more wine. "Guess I pictured you as… I don't know, more of a house-in-a-residential-neighborhood-type city dweller."

"That's not too far off the mark." He gave another laugh. "I'm pretty close to all the city action. But I'm also a country boy, having grown up on a sprawling ranch in Oklahoma."

"Interesting." Abby regarded him for a long moment. "Where did you meet your ex-wife?"

The question took Scott by surprise, but he quickly recovered. "In Kentucky… Lexington," he answered, wondering where this was going.

She sat back. "What happened to cause the marriage to end, if you don't mind my asking?"

Even more direct. But he didn't fault her for it. Scott saw this as part of the process of getting to know someone, in spite of the regrets he had in seeing his marriage blow up. "I don't mind," he said sincerely, touching the wineglass but not drinking from it. "We were relatively young when we married and, unfortunately, seemed to lose our way as time progressed. Neither of us really knew how to get back there and decided it was best to call it quits."

Abby met his eyes steadily. "Ever wish you could have a redo? I mean, hindsight is twenty-twenty, as they say. A second chance to iron out the wrinkles maybe?"

Though amused with the clever probing as if to see if he could somehow end up back with his ex instead of a clear willingness to take a chance on someone else, Scott held her gaze and replied in earnest, "No. We had a good marriage for a time, but I have no desire to replay the stress and strain we put on ourselves. Nor will I allow past faults to frighten me from putting myself out there again. Especially when I now have a clean slate and can try to get it right with someone else."

"Hmm…" Her voice had a catch to it as she

finished off her wine. "Hope you like home-made apple pie?"

"I love apple pie," he told her, grinning.

"Me too."

Moments later in the kitchen, they were eating slices of pie, which Scott found just as scrumptious as the main course. In fact, admittedly, there wasn't anything he didn't like about Abby Zhang, with cooking right up there among her qualities. Along with the courage to get past a terrible crime that had forever altered her life. To say nothing about her looks and coolheadedness. So how had she managed to remain single?

He sliced into another piece of pie and asked interestedly, "When was your last relationship?" Had someone turned her off from dating? Or was she just very picky?

"A few months ago." Abby set her plate on the breakfast bar. "A banking executive, his name's Steven Leclerc, and he was way too full of himself for me."

"That's not a good thing in making a relationship work," Scott had to admit, putting his own plate down.

"Right? On top of that, he just wasn't what I was looking for in terms of having the right stuff for true boyfriend material."

"What might that stuff be?" Scott gave her a curious eye.

"Oh, nothing unreachable," she clarified. "Integrity, open-mindedness, no commitment phobias, and a willingness to meet me halfway and see where it can go."

"Sounds more than reasonable to me," he told her intently.

Abby gazed at him. "You think?"

"Yeah. You deserve at least that much from a partner." *So do I*, Scott thought.

"We all do," she stressed.

He looked at Abby's beautiful face and reached out to a corner of her mouth. "There's a little crumb there." He gladly removed it and flicked it onto her plate.

She blushed. "Thanks."

Scott felt this was the perfect moment to do what he had been wanting to do for some time. Were they on the same page? He lifted her chin up, tilted his own face and, while staring into Abby's eyes, slowly leaned forward till he was certain she had no objections, and gently kissed her lips. They were as soft as he could have imagined.

Better yet was when Abby deepened the kiss and Scott happily went with it, feeling her heartbeat. Or was it his own?

After a few minutes of kissing, Scott forced himself to pull back. "I should probably go," he told her reluctantly.

Abby touched her swollen mouth. "Okay."

Though he relished the thought of making love to her, Scott had decided it best to take things slow, so as not to blow what had the potential of becoming something special.

After she walked him out, he told her, "I'll let you know what I learn about Gilliard."

She nodded. "Okay."

"Thanks again for the dinner and dessert. They were great." He smiled. "Hopefully, you'll let me return the favor sometime."

Abby smiled back. "Whenever you like."

Scott took that to heart and immediately began to make tentative plans to play host to her for a meal as he climbed into his Ford Explorer and drove off.

Chapter Seven

On Friday morning, Scott was up bright and early to exercise his horse while still on a high from kissing Abby last evening. He saw that as a positive sign for what could become a regular thing for them and so much more. Having failed at this once before did not mean he couldn't correct his mistakes in the future, with the help of the right woman in his life. Maybe that would be Abby.

After half an hour of riding, Scott drove to work. Inside the field office, he gave his boss, Diane Huggett, a brief update on the cold case investigation, got limited feedback and headed to his office. Sitting at his desk, he got on the laptop and ran a criminal background check on Zach Gilliard. Aside from a couple of parking tickets and a minor drug offense from fifteen years ago, he was clean. At least officially. Though there was no record of stalking or harassment, it didn't mean there was no history there. Or, more specifically, that he hadn't chosen Abby to become his first stalking victim.

Scott grabbed his cell phone from the pocket of his pants and called Detective Selena Nunez. She answered after one ring and said, "Agent Lynley."

"Detective. I need a favor."

"Sure. How can I help you?"

"I need to know if a Zach Gilliard was at the police department yesterday afternoon, donating some items," Scott told her.

"Let me check the log on that," she responded.

"Okay."

A minute later, Selena came back on the line. "Yeah, Gilliard did donate some used clothing and books in the afternoon for us to distribute to those in need," she confirmed. "Why do you ask?"

"I was looking into a possible stalking incident," Scott explained, leaving it at that.

"So, how are you doing on the cold case?"

"Still a work in progress," he admitted. "Following leads as they come."

"Well, keep at it," Selena urged. "No one would like to see this case solved more than myself. Short of Abby Zhang."

I'm just as keen on that, Scott thought. "Will do."

After disconnecting, he opened the Veronica

Liu file and found the info on Oliver Dillman. Not too much. Dillman, thirty-seven at the time and divorced, once questioned, had produced an alibi and had no longer been considered a suspect worth focusing on. Was that a mistake?

Scott took a deeper look at the primary suspects in the Liu homicide: Evan Liu, the ex-husband; Mathew Yang, the boyfriend; Katlyn Johansson, the possibly vindictive exotic dancer; and Bennie Romero, a wanderer with a meth-amphetamine addiction. Could one of those four have been responsible for Veronica's death?

Let's see if any or all are still alive today, Scott told himself, as a starting point. He went on the computer and accessed official and public databases. Going with Bennie Romero first, Scott learned that he had died of a drug overdose a decade ago. Still didn't mean he wasn't Veronica's killer, but he had found a way to escape justice.

Pulling up information on the other three suspects, as near as Scott could determine, all were alive and well and still living within the greater Bluegrass region of Kentucky. Good. Reinterrogating them, along with Oliver Dillman, could yield results. Or not.

His train of thought was interrupted by a video chat request on his computer from his sister Madison. Now Madison Lynley-Sneed, she was a law enforcement ranger in the Pisgah Ranger District, located in the Pisgah National Forest in North Carolina. She had recently wed National Park Service Investigative Services Branch Special Agent Garrett Sneed.

Scott accepted the chat and watched as Madison, two years his junior, appeared on the screen. "Hi."

"Hi, big brother." Bold aquamarine eyes beamed at him on an attractive face surrounded by long blond hair in a shaggy wolf cut with curly bangs. "Got a minute?"

He grinned. "I'm sure I can spare a couple," he joked. "What's up?"

"I need some advice," she told him with a catch to her voice.

"Okay." Scott braced himself for whatever was to come, while always happy to know that his younger siblings wanted his guidance.

Madison waited a beat then said, "I've been asked to conduct a seminar for the National Park Service Law Enforcement Training Center at Southwestern Community College."

"Sounds good," he said, sensing more to the story.

"Thing is, it conflicts with my working with kids on how to become a Blue Ridge Parkway junior ranger," she complained, her duties mostly within the Blue Ridge Mountains. "Sort of had my mind set on that. With Garrett away on assignment, well…what do you think?"

"I think you should go with your instincts on what works best for you at this time." Scott realized that was probably taking the easy way out, but he stood by it. "There will be other seminars, I'm sure. But it's always nice to encourage children to follow in your footsteps."

"Okay." She took a breath. "Thanks, as always, for being straight with me and a listening ear to your sister."

He grinned. "Happy to help, Madison."

She giggled. "So, what are you up to? Oh, wait," she uttered. "Russell mentioned a little about your latest cold case investigation. And a little girl left behind." Madison paused. "How's it going?"

"That little girl's not so little anymore," he couldn't help but point out, thinking about the kiss they'd shared. "But she's managed to move on with her life."

Madison nodded. "That's a good thing."

"Yeah." Scott leaned forward. "Regarding the case, as you might expect when we're talking about decades-old cases, the devil is in the details, which I'm still trying to piece together," he told her. He thought about the one sure bright spot in the investigation, getting to meet Abby, a definite breath of fresh air as far as he was concerned. "I'm getting there. Or trying to."

She smiled. "Well, I for one have the utmost confidence in you, Scott. We all know that when any of the Lynleys set his or her mind to something, there's no stopping us."

He laughed. "Spoken like a true Lynley." That, their parents would have approved of wholeheartedly.

They ended the conversation with plans to talk again soon.

Scott headed out for his first interview of the day. During the drive, he called Abby and put her on speakerphone. "Hey."

"Hi," she said cheerfully.

"I wanted to let you know that Zach Gilliard's story checked out," Scott told her. "He logged in to drop off items at the police station around the time he claimed to. No record of any serious offenses either."

"That's good to know." She sighed. "Guess it means Zach wasn't stalking me."

"Looks that way." Scott wasn't entirely convinced that the man's behavior in sending flowers anonymously and following her to the cemetery was on the up-and-up. But he wouldn't make a big deal out of it, frightening Abby unnecessarily. "Keep an eye out nevertheless for any indication to the contrary."

"I will," she promised.

"I'm on my way to speak with suspects in the original investigation into your aunt's murder," he told her.

"You really think one of them could have killed her and outfoxed the investigators at the time?" Abby questioned.

"Wouldn't be the first time a suspect had managed to delay justice for years." Scott switched lanes. "Whatever the case, I'll see what they have to say for themselves today and go from there."

"Good luck."

"I won't stop searching for answers, Abby. I hope you know that," he felt the need to say.

"I do, Scott," she assured him, "and thank you."

He paused. "It was a nice kiss."

"I agree." She took a long moment. "We should try it again sometime."

"I'd like that." He gazed out the windshield thoughtfully. "I'll see you later."

"All right."

After he ended the chat, Scott couldn't help but crack a grin as he envisioned what it would be like to make love to Abby. The fact that she seemed into him, too, made it all the more exciting. The most important thing to him was that he not allow past mistakes to define the future and its endless possibilities. Were they on the same trajectory?

THE KISS THAT was short and oh, so sweet had admittedly still been on Abby's mind even before Scott had brought it up as she disconnected her cell phone after chatting with him. She was sitting at her desk, wondering if this truly could be the start of something great. Or would it end up being another big disappointment when it came to romance in her life? She wasn't hedging her bets either way as yet, vowing to keep an open mind on Scott. Just as she was on his ability to solve a case that had grown ice-cold over two decades, where others before him had failed.

Her reverie came to a halt when Abby's boss, Darren Jordache, the supervisory senior resident agent in charge of the FBI's Owensboro satellite office, walked in. African American and in his late thirties, he was tall and good-looking, with short black hair in a line-up cut, a pencil mustache and brown eyes.

"Hi, Darren."

"Hi." He gave her a grim-faced look. "There's been a school bus incident on Highway 54."

"Oh, no," she uttered, fearing the worst. "What happened?"

"An armed murder suspect, Roy Lamb, hopped on the bus, filled with children, and killed the driver, a fifty-nine-year-old grandmother named Marissa Heigl. The Bureau's Hostage Rescue Team ended up killing Lamb

after he threatened to start shooting students."
Jordache grimaced. "Unfortunately, the bus
crashed, flipping once. Dozens of students have
been hospitalized," he told her. "Fortunately,
none have life-threatening injuries."

"Thank goodness for that." Abby breathed
a sigh of relief, though saddened about the bus
driver's death. "What hospital?"

"You mean hospitals." Jordache mentioned
the three local hospitals they'd been sent to.
"Elise is already coordinating services for victims at two hospitals. I need you to head over
to Kolton Lake General and see what they need
in moving forward."

She got to her feet and told him, "I'm on my
way."

He nodded. "This could've been a lot worse."

"I know," she said, having seen as much first-
hand in her work.

Two hours later, Abby had provided resources
to students, all of whom had been released from
the hospital, and their parents, while reassuring
them that the Bureau's victim services would
continue to be available for as long as needed.

But when she was about to leave, Abby
could have sworn that she saw Zach Gilliard
at the end of the corridor. Had she imagined
it? Had he followed her to the hospital? Probably against her better judgment, she moved to-

ward him. Seemingly at the same time, the man began to head away from her, as if in a hurry to evade detection. By the time she reached the area, he was gone.

Had it really been Zach? Was he stalking her, in spite of Scott suggesting that he wasn't a threat?

Or have I allowed myself to get worked up over nothing? She decided that was probably the case. Even if Zach were there, he could have been visiting someone. And may not have even been aware of her presence.

She sucked in a deep breath and headed in the opposite direction. Impulsively, though, she looked over her shoulder. As if expecting Zach—or the man in question—to have resurfaced. But there was no one there.

SCOTT PULLED UP to the Dutch Colonial house on Wrightmoore Drive, where he'd learned that Oliver Dillman was doing a showing. Parked in the driveway was a silver Lexus UX 200 and a blue Acura Integra.

After a young couple left the two-story residence, and got into the Integra and drove off, with or without the sale being made, Scott left his SUV and went inside the house. He found the man he was looking for shutting things down in the roomy, staged home in the formal living room that had plenty of windows and a large, welcoming fireplace.

Recognizing Dillman from his website photograph, Scott studied him briefly. He was in his late fifties, over six feet tall, and sturdy enough in business casual attire and leather loafers. His salt-and-pepper short hair was wavy with a side part. Scott cleared his throat to gain the man's attention.

"Sorry, didn't hear you come in." Dillman, who had just closed the living room drapes, favored him with blue eyes. "You here for a showing?"

"Not exactly." Though Scott imagined it was a place he could live in were he in the market. "Oliver Dillman?" he asked knowingly, approaching across the oak hardwood flooring.

"Yeah, I'm Oliver Dillman." He met him halfway. "Who are you?"

Scott removed his identification, flashing it as he said, "FBI Special Agent Lynley."

Dillman cocked a thick brow. "What does an FBI agent want to see me about?"

"I've reopened the investigation into the murder of Veronica Liu," Scott told him levelly.

"Veronica Liu?" Dillman reacted to the name. "Haven't heard that name in years," he claimed. His brow furrowed. "Again, what does this have to do with me?"

Scott locked eyes with him. "Your name came up in the course of my reexamining the case, as one of the original persons questioned in relation to her death. I'd like to go over your statements and relationship to Ms. Liu."

"I'd be happy to tell you anything I can recall about Veronica, Agent Lynley, but I'm in a bit of a hurry," he argued. "I have another showing across town."

"I understand," Scott said succinctly. "I have no problem arranging a time for you to come down to the FBI field office to talk. Or we can do it now. Your call."

Dillman regarded him thoughtfully for a few moments and said, "Maybe it is best to get this over with now." He paused. "What would you like to know?"

Scott got right to it. "Did you have anything to do with Ms. Liu's murder?" he asked bluntly.

"Absolutely not!" Dillman insisted with a straight face. "I had an alibi for when Veronica was murdered."

"Which was?" Scott wanted to test his memory.

After a moment or two, he responded smoothly, "It was a long time ago, but as I recall, I was on the road in between showing houses and nowhere near Veronica's house."

"Had you ever been to her cabin?" Scott asked him.

"No," he replied flatly. "She never invited me over, so I had no reason to go there."

"Maybe your reason was that you didn't take rejection lightly and were more than willing to force the issue, if you didn't get what you wanted from her."

"Rejection? What?" Dillman's face tightened. "Who told you I was rejected by her?"

"Are you denying that you hit on Ms. Liu and she told you she wasn't interested?" Scott peered at him. "Or that you were fired from the real estate office because you went after another female agent who also rebuffed your ill-advised advances?"

Dillman did an about-face. "Okay, you got me. I did hit on Veronica and others at the agency who I was attracted to. I admit, I was a bit of a jerk back in those days. And it cost me my job. But I certainly wasn't so desperate as to murder someone simply because she wouldn't go out with me. To suggest otherwise, Agent Lynley, would be barking up the wrong tree."

"If you say so." Scott wasn't entirely convinced he was as innocent as he claimed to be. But there was simply no evidence at this time to indicate otherwise. "When you worked with

Ms. Liu, were you aware of anyone else who may have wished her harm?"

Dillman rubbed his jaw. "No one comes to mind," he answered. "Whoever killed Veronica, I doubt it had anything to do with her being a Realtor. She was a capable agent who knew how to close the deal, and was respected by her agents in the office and competitors alike, as far as I knew." He waited a beat and said, "I'd heard that she was seeing some guy who was two-timing her. Whether that had anything to do with Veronica's death, I have no idea."

Neither do I, Scott reflected, knowing that the person in question was her former boyfriend, Mathew Yang. *But I intend to find out.* "That should do it, for now," he told Dillman.

He nodded. "Hope you solve the case, Agent Lynley. Believe it or not, I feel just as bad as anyone that Veronica was murdered twenty years ago. She really was a damned good real estate agent and taught me a thing or two that I've carried with me to this day in the selling of houses."

"Nice to know." Scott gazed at him. "I can see myself out."

He left on that note, not believing Oliver Dillman should be moved up the list of suspects any more now than two decades ago. Unless circumstances should present themselves in rethinking that.

Chapter Eight

Scott stepped into the roomy office of Mathew Yang, who was the chief financial officer of the public relations firm Suehiro and Iwalani Communications, operating out of a high-rise on Fullerton Street in downtown Kolton Lake. Yang, who was in his midfifties and slender, with short black hair in a comb-over style, approached Scott.

"Special Agent Lynley, I take it," Yang said, regarding him with sable eyes behind wire-rimmed glasses.

Scott nodded. "Yes."

"Mathew Yang." He put out a hand. "Nice to meet you." After Scott shook his hand, Yang said, "I have to admit that it threw me for a loop when you said over the phone that you were re-opening the case into Veronica's death."

"It was something that needed to happen," Scott told him tersely. "Just happened to fall in my lap and I plan to see it through."

"I understand." Yang looked away. "Why don't we sit?"

He led him to a pair of leather wing chairs by a floor-to-ceiling window. After Scott sat, he said straightforwardly, "I'm reinterviewing everyone who was considered a suspect in the original investigation. Given the nature of your relationship at the time with Ms. Liu, while being married to another woman, you were obviously at the top of the list."

"I was also cleared of playing any role in Veronica's death," he pointed out.

Scott struck back. "That was then, this is now. You'll need to convince me that you're innocent of any wrongdoing in Ms. Liu's murder to take you off the front burners."

Yang ran a hand across his mouth uneasily. "Look, I'm not proud of the way I handled things with Veronica," he contended. "But I didn't kill her. I was in love with Veronica and planned to ask her to marry me, once I got a divorce."

"From what I understand, Ms. Liu never even knew you were already married." Scott eyed him sharply. "If this is incorrect, now's the time to say so."

"It's true." Yang drew a deep breath. "I never got the chance to confess this to Veronica before she was killed. But I had every intention of doing so. My marriage was in name only. We weren't even living together anymore. Once it became untenable, my then wife, Loretta, and I agreed to go our separate ways. When I met Veronica, she gave me a new lease on life as far as romance. We started making plans for a future together, which included her niece, Abby." He smoothed a brow musingly. "Never even met her till the funeral. Veronica said she wanted to wait on that till the time was right, so Abby wouldn't have another letdown in her life."

"But that ended up happening anyway," Scott said sadly, "when someone decided to murder Veronica Liu."

"It wasn't me," Yang insisted. "I was at work at the time, with witnesses. Believe me when I tell you, Agent Lynley, it tore me to pieces when I got the news that Veronica was dead."

So you say, Scott mused, knowing that the alibi had checked out. "What about your wife?" he pressed. "Was she as broken up about it?"

"As I said, we were estranged and Loretta no longer concerned herself about my love life," he argued. "Or vice versa."

Scott had heard all that before and found that, in many instances, one side or the other was reluctant to see the marriage end. To the contrary, more often than not, a spouse who was being cheated on wasn't very happy about the adultery. Jealous rage came to mind. Was that the case here? Could it have resulted in a revenge killing, in spite of the original investigation that concluded otherwise?

"I'd like to speak with your ex," Scott told him. "Get her side of this…"

"I'm afraid that won't be possible." Yang touched his glasses. "Loretta died of ovarian cancer eight years ago."

"I see." Scott wondered if she could have taken any relevant secrets with her to the grave.

"Neither of us had anything to do with what happened to Veronica," he asserted. "You have to believe that, Agent Lynley. Even after all these years, the idea that I could have harmed one hair on the head of someone I loved still pains me."

Scott sensed his sincerity, but continued to consider him a person of interest. "That should be all, for now." He rose.

"I suppose you've spoken with Abby?" Yang asked, standing.

"I have," Scott admitted.

"How's she doing?" His voice lowered an octave.

"As well as one could expect when having to relive a painful chapter in her life," he told him candidly.

"Many times, I've wanted to reach out to her, but just wasn't sure how."

"Maybe you'll figure it out," Scott said equably, knowing he would leave it up to Mathew and Abby as to if and when they'd want to get together.

Yang nodded. "Yeah, maybe."

Scott left the public relations firm with Veronica's ex-husband, Evan Liu, next up to be reinterviewed in trying to track down the killer of Abby's aunt.

AFTER WORK, Abby sat outside her cabin by the lake with her friend Phoebe Hoag on saucer chairs. She had known Phoebe since childhood and had kept in touch with her over the years, in spite of taking different paths in life, before both had resettled in Kolton Lake.

Phoebe, also thirty-two and a neurologist at Kolton Lake General, was gorgeous, with long chestnut hair in an A-line style and baby blue eyes. Just as slender as Abby and a little taller, Phoebe was fresh off a divorce from her college sweetheart and dating a cardiologist. While sipping beer, they talked about the recent school bus accident and fortunate passengers. Abby chose not to bring up the possible sighting of Zach Gilliard at the hospital, fearing Phoebe might think she was losing her mind. And Abby wondered if she might not agree, given what she had learned about him from Scott and having no further direct contact with Zach since seeing him at the cemetery.

Afterward, Abby told her friend about the reopening of the investigation into her aunt Veronica's murder.

"Seriously?" Phoebe fluttered her lashes in shock. "After all these years?"

"I know." Abby was still pinching herself to believe it was really happening. She remembered that she had sat beside Phoebe on the school bus that day, before Phoebe had been let off one stop earlier than she had. Abby could only imagine if it had been her friend who'd discovered her mother murdered in her own car in the driveway. "FBI Special Agent Scott Lynley decided it was a case worth pursuing." His pursuit of her or vice versa was something Abby had not expected either.

"Has he made any progress?"

"I suppose," Abby answered matter-of-factly. "He's talking to people who knew my aunt, original witnesses and suspects, looking at evidence, et cetera. But these things take time in such an old case." She understood, tempering her enthusiasm for good results, if not for the handsome agent himself.

Phoebe made a face. "I really hope this Agent

Lynley makes a breakthrough in finally solving the crime," she voiced.

"Me too." Abby lifted the beer bottle. "Aunt Veronica has waited long enough for the world to learn what she had to have known herself but was no longer able to communicate to anyone in the living world."

"I agree." Phoebe put the beer bottle to her glossy lips. "So, other than you and Jeanne Singletary, just how many people are still around who actually remember your aunt and can assist in the investigation?"

"Well, there's my aunt's ex, Evan Liu, and former lover, Mathew Yang," Abby told her, knowing they had continued to live in the area, though she didn't have a relationship with either. "Then there's Mayor Freda Myerson."

"Really?" Phoebe's sculpted brows shot up. "Mayor Myerson knew your aunt?"

"I guess not that well, but Aunt Veronica did sell the mayor her first home, when she was still just Freda Neville twenty-plus years ago."

"Who knew?" Phoebe chuckled. "I read once that Mayor Myerson had been married at least twice, had her fair share of wealthy boyfriends along the way, and was known to be a real reveler back in the day. That was before she settled down with her current husband, philanthropist Pierce Myerson, and turned her attention to becoming mayor of Kolton Lake, with an eye for higher political office."

"At least my aunt brushed shoulders with her way back when," Abby quipped while glancing at the lake. "In case Freda should someday decide to run for president."

"You never know." Phoebe giggled and drank beer. "In any event, let's keep our fingers crossed that the FBI agent knows what he's doing in taking on the case."

"Yeah, let's." Abby crossed her fingers for effect then said thoughtfully, "Speaking of Agent Lynley—Scott... I kind of have the hots for him and the feeling seems mutual."

"Oh, really?" Phoebe grinned. "Do tell."

Abby kept it short and sweet, knowing that she and Scott had barely scratched the surface, though enough to give her an itch as to the potential for a relationship with the special agent. She finished by revealing to her friend that they'd kissed.

"Hmm..." Phoebe's voice rose excitedly. "Can't wait to see if one thing will lead to another."

"Neither can I," Abby admitted while staying grounded should things not go that way.

"You deserve someone in your life who can actually prove to be more than the self-absorbed, undependable and otherwise bad-news types that have entered and exited your life over the years."

"Tell me something I don't already know." Abby chuckled and sipped the beer. "On second thought, don't tell me. I'll just have to live and learn whether there's something worth pursuing or not with Scott Lynley."

Phoebe smiled and clinked their beer bottles. "Fair enough."

In her head, Abby already believed it to be worthwhile. She just wouldn't put the cart ahead of the horse. But was more than ready to get in the saddle should she be invited to do so.

Scott rang the bell of the lodge-style house in the affluent town of Kolton Hills, adjacent to Kolton Lake, where Evan Liu resided on Benes Lane. A white BMW Alpina XB7 was parked in the driveway. The front door of the home opened and a dark-haired young woman wearing a housekeeping uniform stood there.

"Can I help you?" she asked.

"I'd like to see Evan Liu," he told her.

Her brown eyes regarded him curiously. "Is Mr. Liu expecting you?"

"Not exactly." Scott met her gaze. "I'm with the FBI. It's official business."

"Just a moment." She left him standing there for about a minute. When she came back, Scott was told, "Mr. Liu will see you. He's in his garden. You can go around the house and meet him there."

"Thanks," Scott said, and proceeded to follow a well-manicured path till he spotted a slender man in his early sixties, with short gray hair, wearing garden gloves while tending to some perennial plants. He stopped when Scott walked across the grass toward him.

"I'm Evan Liu," he said curiously, wiping his brow with the back of his hand.

"Special Agent Lynley," Scott told him, showing his identification.

Behind oval glasses, Liu trained black eyes on him. "What does an FBI agent need to see a retired pharmacist about?"

"Your ex-wife, Veronica Liu," Scott responded directly. "I've reopened the investigation into her murder."

"Really?" Liu's voice rang with surprise. "That happened so long ago."

"I'm a cold case investigator," Scott told him, wondering if he had been in touch with Abby. "No homicide is ever so long ago that we simply sweep it under the rug."

"I understand," he said lowly.

"Especially one that was inexplicable while shattering the life of your niece, Abby Zhang," Scott thought to add.

Liu stiffened. "How is she?"

"Abby is as well as could be expected when having to go through the ordeal again of her aunt's death." Scott met his stare. "She works for the FBI now as a victim specialist, in case you didn't know."

"I didn't," he confessed. "We stopped communicating after Veronica and I divorced. My mistake."

Scott agreed, but wasn't there to help Evan Liu make amends, though he was welcome to do so. Assuming he wasn't responsible for the tragedy she'd had to endure. "I'd like to ask you a few questions pertaining to Veronica Liu's death."

"Okay." Liu pursed his lips. "But just so you know, I had nothing to do with what happened to my ex-wife. We were divorced for two years when she was killed. The police at the time verified my alibi."

"So they did," Scott acknowledged. "It also came to light that your relationship with Veronica was strained and the divorce not entirely amicable. In my book, that leaves open the possibility that you might have wanted your ex-wife dead in an 'if I can't have you, no one can' kind of way. If true, it wouldn't have been unthinkable that you could have hired someone else to do your dirty work for you."

"Nonsense!" Liu shot back. "I'm sure you're just doing your job, Agent Lynley, but any suggestion that I could have used a hired killer to murder someone I had distanced myself from makes no sense."

"Murder rarely does make sense," Scott countered. "Particularly where it concerns matters of the heart. Being manipulative and vengeful can make people do crazy things."

"Not me," he snorted. "I admit that my marriage to Veronica was less than perfect. But it wasn't all my fault. We both made errors in judgment and it cost us the relationship. Was I happy that she kicked me out? No. But I got over it and learned from my mistakes. I fell in love with someone else and we're still going strong more than two decades later." Liu sighed. "As for Veronica, I'm sorry that someone murdered her. But it wasn't me. I knew how much she loved that little girl, Abby, after losing her own parents at such a young age. I would never have taken Veronica away from her, adding to Abby's sad childhood and beyond."

He struck Scott as legit enough in his tone. It was on that basis that he told Evan Liu he was off the hook as of now as a suspect in his ex-wife's death. But if he needed to work his way back around to Liu, Scott was more than prepared to do so. He allowed him to return to his gardening and Scott left the same way he came.

THAT EVENING, Scott walked into the Loren's Club, a nightclub on Dentry Avenue in Bowling Green where Katlyn Johansson worked as a bartender. He made his way through the crowd till he found the man he was looking for, Art Reilly, of the Bureau's Bowling Green resident agency.

"Hey," Scott said to him.

Reilly, who was nursing a drink at the bar, replied, "There you are. Was beginning to think I'd been stood up."

"Not a chance." Scott chuckled. "Sorry I'm late. I was delayed in the process of my investigation."

"Don't worry about it." He finished off the drink. "You're still buying, right?"

"Absolutely." Scott sat beside him. "The next one's on me."

Reilly nodded and regarded him with curiosity. "So, why am I here?"

"Well, as you know, I'm reinterviewing original suspects in the Veronica Liu homicide," Scott explained.

"Yeah?"

"One of them, Katlyn Johansson, happens to work in this very bar," he told him. "Since it's right in your neck of the woods, figured you might want to step into the ring with me in talking with her. Just in case it triggers something that I might miss."

"Okay, I'm game." Reilly rubbed his chin pensively. "Where is she?"

"Right there." Scott shifted his eyes toward the bartender who had presumably served Reilly his first drink. And was now headed their way.

Katlyn Johansson was in her midforties, medium size, and had a black bob with fuchsia highlights worn in a peekaboo hairstyle. She peered at Scott with blue eyes and said, "What can I get you?"

"A few minutes of your time." He fixed on her face. "Are you Katlyn Johansson?" he asked, though already knowing the answer from having done his homework.

"Who's asking?"

Scott flashed his ID. "FBI Special Agent Lynley."

She cocked a thin brow and favored Reilly. "Supervisory Senior Agent Reilly," he said tonelessly. "You may not remember me but—"

"I thought you looked familiar," Katlyn said. "We spoke years ago when you were investigating the murder of..."

"Veronica Liu," he told her.

"Yeah, that's right."

Scott leaned forward and said, "I've reopened the case."

"Really?" She cocked a brow. "And you want to question me again about it?"

"Just need to go over your original statement as part of the routine investigation," he claimed. "We can do it now or…"

"Go ahead." Katlyn rested her hands on the counter. "I have nothing to hide."

"If my memory serves me correctly," Reilly told her, scratching his pate, "you had words with Ms. Liu at the Tygers Club on Third Street, where you were working at the time, the night before she was killed. Do you recall what that was all about?"

Katlyn stared at him for an instant and replied thoughtfully, "Sure. It was just a misunderstanding. Back then, when I had a badass body as a dancer, men liked to ogle me while on stage. As I remember it, one of those was a guy Veronica Liu was with. She seemed to think I was hitting on him through the dancing, I guess. And let me know afterward to lay off her man. I didn't take too kindly to being accused of something I was innocent of and let her know this. That was about it."

"Actually, according to witnesses," Scott pointed out, "you followed Ms. Liu outside the establishment, seemingly itching for a fight.

So how far were you willing to take this?" he questioned.

"The witnesses got it wrong," she insisted. "I only went out to get some air. By then, Veronica was already gone. I never saw or spoke to her again, I swear." Katlyn took a breath. "Next thing I knew, I heard that she was shot to death and I was being interrogated about it by the cops…and you, Agent Reilly. And I'm no more guilty today of killing her than I was two decades ago."

"Sure about that?" Reilly asked, glaring at her, but with a tone that suggested he believed it to be true.

"Yeah. Committing cold-blooded murder to settle an imaginary romantic triangle is going overboard. Don't you think?"

Reilly tugged at his mustache and looked at Scott before saying, "She's still a weak link in the chain."

He was inclined to agree, but Scott had to ask the bartender, "Did you own a gun back then?"

"No." Katlyn shook her head. "I hate guns and would never own one."

"Okay." Scott realized that this was going nowhere with her. Then something that could only be called a long shot entered his head. "Do you happen to recall if there was anyone else at the bar that night who Veronica Liu may have had a beef with? Or otherwise got on the bad side of?" There was no record of such in the original report. Could it have been overlooked?

Katlyn pondered this. "It was so long ago…" She pressed her lips together. "I think Veronica may have exchanged words with another guy when her boyfriend was preoccupied with me. I can't be sure."

"Do you remember anything about this man?" Scott asked interestedly. "Age, race, size, hairstyle, et cetera."

"Definitely white, dark-haired and average size," she responded. "Can't remember any more than that, sorry." Just as swiftly, Katlyn uttered, "Now that I think about it, I had the feeling that they weren't strangers to one another. Don't ask me why. Anyway, I need to get back to work."

Scott nodded. He took out his wallet and put money on the counter, which included a nice tip, and said, "Why don't you give Agent Reilly here a refill?"

"All right." Katlyn looked at Scott. "What about you?"

He waved her off. "I'm good."

After briefly conferring with the supervisory senior special agent, who seemed to think this unsub was a nothing burger, Scott respectfully had to disagree. "All leads are worth pursuing, no matter how long the odds of hitting pay dirt."

Reilly didn't argue the point. "You're right. We obviously missed something in the equation. Check it out, see what you come up with. It's your case now, Lynley, and I'm pulling for you."

Scott accepted that from him for what it was worth, thanking Reilly for showing up, before leaving him at the bar as Scott headed home. During the drive, he couldn't help but wonder if, in fact, Veronica Liu had been targeted by someone she'd known at the club that night. If so, who? And what could have triggered such an act of violence?

It left Scott with more food for thought. And an even greater determination to get to the bottom of why Abby's aunt had been shot to death, for her to sadly discover.

Chapter Nine

On Saturday, Abby went for a morning swim. Lake Kolton was gorgeous and the water warm. Only a few boats were out. She wondered if Scott was a swimmer. Or did he prefer riding horses as a good substitute? She began with a front crawl before moving into a backstroke and finishing up with the butterfly as she made her way to shore, feeling tired and energized at the same time.

Out of the water, the blue one-piece swimsuit clung to her like a second skin as she gazed back at the lake and envisioned a time when she'd gone swimming there with her aunt Veronica. It was one of the ways in which they'd bonded and Abby missed the most. At least the memories of the good times would stay with her, even if the tragedy of her aunt's death would as well.

Inside the cabin, Abby dried off and changed into shorts and a square-necked tank top, remaining barefoot as she did some house chores and thought about Scott. She wondered how he was progressing in the investigation and whether or not one thing could truly lead to another in finding a killer who had eluded other investigators for two decades. Her thoughts wandered to the prospects for them beyond the cold case. Were the feelings she was starting to develop for him real? And were they reciprocated from his end beyond a nice kiss they'd shared?

When her cell phone rang, Abby saw that it was Scott calling, as though he had been reading her mind. She answered. "Hello."

"Hi." He paused. "If you're not busy this afternoon, I wanted to return the favor of your incredible meal by inviting you to dinner at my place."

Abby grinned. "I'd love to come to dinner and check out your place."

"Great." He gave her the address and said, "Should be easy to find."

"Okay." As she had GPS in her car, Abby was sure she would have no problem there. "Do you want me to bring anything?"

"Only yourself."

She laughed. "I think I can handle that."

"Actually, now that you mention it, if you're up for riding a horse, you might want to dress accordingly."

"I'm up for it," Abby told him. "Not very experienced in that department, but I did ride a few times when living in the Bay Area."

"Good to know," Scott said. "See you later."

"'Bye." Abby disconnected. She felt almost giddy at another opportunity to spend quality time with Scott. Whether it would lead to them taking things up a notch, if not beyond that, she wasn't sure. She would play it by ear and go with the flow, wherever it led.

A couple of hours later, Abby was driving east on US Route 60 toward Scott's house. She wondered if he was any more comfortable living alone than she was. Or had his divorce soured him on sharing his space with someone else?

She glanced into the rearview mirror nonchalantly and Abby thought she spotted a dark SUV that she had noticed pull onto the highway after she'd entered it from Kolton Lake. There was another car in between them. Yet she was almost certain that it was the same SUV. Was it following her?

She couldn't see the driver. Was it Zach Gilliard? Had she seen him at the hospital yesterday? Or was this whole stalking thing only her imagination probably going too far?

Get a grip, Abby ordered herself. Why would someone be following her the ninety or so miles from Kolton Lake to Louisville? But would distance truly matter to a crazy stalker bent on crowding or attacking, if not killing, her?

Abby changed lanes to see if the SUV did. Or if it would give her a better look at the driver. But the SUV made no attempt to follow her lead. When another car slid in front of the SUV, putting even more of a barrier between it and her, Abby considered that maybe she had once again allowed her imagination to run wild.

By the time she had exited the highway and watched the SUV continue on, Abby realized it had indeed all been in her head. She breathed a sigh of relief on that score. The last thing she needed was to visit Scott with shaky thoughts about a stalker and one who, had the driver been Zach Gilliard, Scott had already assured her, more or less, was no threat to her.

When she drove onto his property, Scott came out to greet her. Between wearing a cowboy hat, a button-down denim shirt, faded jeans and camel-colored leather boots, Abby was seeing him in a whole new, and just as pleasant as before, light. He was grinning broadly. She grinned back and got out of the car.

"Hey, cowboy."

"Hey." He touched the brim of his hat. "Have any trouble finding the place?"

"None whatsoever."

"Good. Dinner's been prepped and will be ready to chow down on in no time flat."

She nodded. "Great, because I'm starving."

"In that case, you've come to the right place." He laughed. "Come on in and I'll show you around."

The tour did not disappoint as Abby marveled at the place the FBI special agent called home. It was spacious, modernized, and seemed to suit him. "I love it," she uttered.

"Thanks." Scott gave a half grin. "I like being able to come back here to chill from the demands of the job."

Abby wondered if that included his current cold case. Not that she could blame him for needing a refuge when having to deal with the lives and deaths typically involved in a criminal investigation. She could say the same when at her log cabin.

"Let's go check out the barn now," he suggested.

"Okay." She smiled. "I'm looking forward to meeting the horses."

They made their way to the four-stall barn, where Scott introduced her to his Thoroughbred, Sammie, and two American Cream Draft horses, named Blaze and Lela. "Later, you can ride Lela, whom I suspect will warm up to you in a hurry."

"I think she already has," Abby said with a chuckle as she rubbed the horse's neck.

"I agree." Scott admired Abby and Lela as he rested a hand on the top of the stall door. "We should go wash up now and then we can eat."

"Sounds good," she told him as they headed back to the house.

To SAY HE wasn't totally turned on by Abby, with her long hair in a ponytail accentuating her attractive face, and dressed for the part on his ranch, would be a flat-out lie. On the contrary, Scott was taken by his guest in ways he had managed to suppress ever since his divorce. Maybe now he had a good reason to bring those emotions back to the surface.

Scott put those carnal thoughts on hold as he stood at the gas grill on his Ipe wood deck, where he was grilling some barbecued pork chops—and veggie burgers to make Abby feel right at home—to go with baked beans, cole-slaw, whole wheat bread and freshly squeezed lemonade. This would be his first time trying the veggie burgers, but he was up for it.

"Dinner is served," Scott declared as he laid it out on the rectangular pine picnic table, where Abby was already seated on the bench.

"Looks delicious," she told him, flashing her teeth.

"Now it's time to see if the taste measures up," he said teasingly, sitting across from her.

Abby wasted little time in taking a bite of the veggie burger. "It's really good."

"Glad you like it." Scott grinned and tried his own burger. "That is tasty and something to add to my food group."

She laughed. "Thanks for being willing to step out of your comfort zone."

"I aim to please," he told her, and meant it where it concerned her.

"Same here." Abby went for a pork chop from the platter. "Mmm, excellent," she said a moment later after taking a bite.

Scott chuckled. "Maybe in my next life, I'll become a chef."

"Why not?" She laughed again and he enjoyed seeing it every time. "And who knows what I'd be? Perhaps a sculptress. Or maybe an engineer."

"I'm sure you would have been successful with any career you put your mind to." He spoke confidently.

"Likewise." She used a napkin to remove barbecue sauce from the corner of her mouth.

Scott spooned some baked beans and asked curiously, "How were things for you living with other relatives in the Bay Area?"

Abby pondered this before responding tranquilly, "Probably as good as could be expected, all things considered. A cousin on my mother's side, Kristin Shao, generously took me in when I had nowhere else to go. But she had her own family and so, while everyone tried their best to make it work out, I never quite felt as if I belonged. Do you know what I mean?"

"Yeah, I can understand that," he told her sincerely, counting his blessings that his family had never been broken while he was still a boy. The fact that Abby had survived her childhood experiences and come out stronger because of them was something to be admired. "What do you remember about your parents?"

"Not too much," she admitted, sipping her lemonade musingly. "I was only six when they passed, but I do recall them being touchy-feely and laughing a lot."

"Good memories to have," he said, even if unable to overcome the darker memories of what was to come in losing them the way she had.

"How about you?" Abby was holding coleslaw on a fork. "Must have been pretty hard losing your parents too?"

"Yeah, it was." Scott drank some lemonade. "I was much older than you when they died in a car accident, but it still took a while to wrap my head around. Both were so full of life, giving, and dedicated to their children and jobs."

"Sounds like they were great people," Abby said. "Wish I had been able to meet them."

"So do I. Mom and Dad would've liked you." He was certain. Just as Scott knew that his siblings would approve of him having Abby in his life.

Abby beamed and ate more of the veggie burgers. She grew more serious when asking, "Have you made any more headway on the investigation into Aunt Veronica's murder?"

Though part of Scott had wanted to avoid talking about the case in this get-together, so as not to dampen the mood, he knew that as long as this elephant was in the room or environment, there was no avoiding it. Moreover, he owed it to Abby to be as straight as he could without compromising the investigation in any way.

"I'm still waiting for the results on the retesting of forensic evidence," he told her, breaking off a piece of wheat bread. "I've been tracking down the original suspects to either eliminate them from further scrutiny or maintain as persons of interest."

She jutted her chin. "I hope there's a break in the case that can blow it wide open in terms of nailing my aunt's killer."

"I want that almost as much as you do, Abby." Scott regarded her across the table. "Every day

I feel as if it's moving in the right direction toward that end. You just have to be patient."

She gave a bob of her head. "Don't mean to rush you. I know you can't just wave a magic wand and solve something twenty years in the making."

"Believe me, I would if I could," he told her, feeling as though he did need to do more to push the envelope further. "That being said, no crime is unsolvable, apart from maybe Jack the Ripper's serial murders of prostitutes in Victorian England. We have a lot of forensic tools and investigative know-how in our favor. Just need to stay the course."

"That's all I can ask for," she offered, smiling at him.

Scott did consider one thing to that effect as he dabbed a napkin to his mouth. "Actually, I was wondering if you happen to remember any men whom your aunt may have been acquainted with at work or outside of, other than her ex-husband, Evan Liu, or boyfriend, Mathew Yang?"

"Hmm." Abby closed her eyes for reflection. "No one comes to mind. My aunt kept me at what she believed to be a safe distance from the men in her life. She was friendly enough with everyone I saw, including the mail carrier, a male neighbor and even one my teachers, Mr.

Pryce. But I wouldn't call any of them an acquaintance, per se. Why do you ask?"

Scott told her about reinterviewing Katlyn Johansson with the original FBI agent on the case, Art Reilly, on hand, and Katlyn's mention of a man whom Veronica was seen talking to in friendly terms possibly the night before she'd died.

Abby gazed at him. "You think this man could have killed Aunt Veronica?"

"Not necessarily," Scott contended, believing that it was a stretch to assume that this person could have been overlooked in the initial investigation as an unsub. But stranger things had happened. "Could have been a misinterpretation by Johansson and nothing more than an innocent exchange between your aunt and this man at the club. We'll see," he told her, leaving it at that.

"If I think of anyone else, I'll let you know," Abby promised.

"Good enough for me." Scott didn't want her to overthink this, any more than he wanted to himself. He'd been in this business long enough to know that the answers to the toughest questions were usually staring you right in the face. He only needed to see this for what it was. "Are you ready to go horseback riding?" he asked Abby.

"Ready as ever," she proclaimed. "Should be fun."

"It will be," he agreed, finishing off the glass of lemonade.

At the stables, Scott put on his Stetson and handed Abby a cowgirl straw hat, saying, "It belongs to my sister Annette, from her last visit. I'm sure she won't mind if you borrow it."

"Okay." Abby grinned and put it atop her head. "Fits perfectly."

He smiled, agreeing totally and liking how the hat looked on her as she posed with it.

They saddled up the horses and Scott helped Abby climb onto the American Cream Draft horse named Lela, and he got on Sammie, his Thoroughbred, before they went on the riding trail and he showed Abby more of the property while feeling that she fit right into his world, apart from both working for the Bureau.

WHEN THEY GOT back to his house forty-five minutes later, Scott poured them both a glass of red wine. Even after taking a few sips of the tasty drink, Abby was clearheaded enough to know that she found the FBI special agent incredibly handsome and sexy. And that she wanted him. Though she was not accustomed to initiating sexual advances, this time she felt like making an exception. Would Scott swallow the bait?

Before she could venture down that road, he kissed her and said desirously, "The wine tastes a lot better coming off your lips."

"Oh, really?" Abby felt even more turned on. "In that case, maybe we need to try that again."

"I'd like nothing better," Scott responded surely. He cupped her cheeks and kissed her again. Abby opened her mouth as the kiss intensified. She stood on her tiptoes and wrapped her hand around his head, taking in his manly scent, arousing her even more as she felt her heartbeat move erratically. "What do you say we take this up to my bedroom?" he asked huskily after pulling back and gazing into her eyes. "Or am I being premature in wanting to go to the next level of what we have going on here?"

"You're not being premature at all, Scott," Abby assured him. "I'm more than ready to move to that next level. Now!"

He beamed lustfully. "Say no more."

Hand in hand, they walked from the chef's kitchen and headed up the winding staircase to the second story. Stepping into the generous primary suite, Abby did a quick scan of the Old World style. It had a vaulted ceiling and interesting angles with an abundance of windows covered by honeycomb shades. The midcentury-modern furniture included a solid wood spindle bed, which she focused on, anticipating getting beneath the blue coverlet with Scott.

Abby turned to him and again fell into a passionate kiss before she broke it off and, with swollen lips, uttered unabashedly, "Let's get naked."

Scott grinned attentively. "The sooner the better."

They practically raced to disrobe and when both were completely in the nude, Abby regarded Scott's rock-hard body, making him even more desirable. She saw him appraising her, as well, making her slightly self-conscious till he said flatly, "You are so hot."

"So are you." Abby prided herself for staying in shape as she pulled her hair out of the ponytail and met his steady gaze. "Do you have protection?" she thought to ask, knowing that even in the face of wanting a man like never before, they still needed to be responsible.

"Yeah," he confirmed, and disappeared into the bathroom briefly. He returned with the condom in place on his erection, and said smoothly, "Now, where were we?"

"About to go to bed." She gulped. "Make love to me, Scott."

"With pleasure and more," he told her, scooping her into his muscular arms and carrying her to the bed, where he lay her down gently before joining her.

As they cuddled and resumed kissing, Scott first ran his fingers through her hair. Then he began caressing her breasts and nipples, driving Abby crazy with delight. "Mmm..." she cooed, nibbling on his lower lip.

"There's more where that came from," he stated, seemingly more than content to take his sweet time with foreplay. Then his hands went farther down and things reached a fever pitch before she could stand the pure torture no more. Through his mouth, she demanded, "I need you inside me!"

"I need that too." Scott kissed her again. "Just want to be sure you're ready. Don't want to rush this."

"I'm ready," Abby said fervently. "It's time!"

As though this triggered a signal in his brain, Scott obeyed her command and positioned himself between her legs, moving deep inside Abby. She was more than welcoming, arching her back and meeting him halfway and then some as her orgasm came almost instantly.

With the shuddering of her body and sounds of satisfaction that escaped Abby, she encouraged Scott, who had clearly been holding back, to join her on the other end. He picked up the pace and she clung to him as he trembled mightily with the powerful release that brought them even closer together.

When it was over, Abby had to say, "It was great." She could have even said "fantastic" or "mind-blowing," but had chosen to restrain herself. Now was probably not the time to get too carried away or emotional.

"More like amazing," Scott said, lying on his back while catching his breath.

She blushed. "You think?"

"I know." He kissed her shoulder. "Some things in life are simply meant to be."

Abby chuckled. "Having sex?"

"Having sex with someone you're in sync with."

"So we're in sync now, are we?"

"Yeah," he said without prelude. "I think you feel it too."

"Hmm…" Abby admittedly was beginning to feel this, as well, as a sense of belonging where it concerned Scott. Were the two one and the same? "I think you're right."

She could only wonder now where things were headed from here. And how far up the ladder they might climb.

Chapter Ten

"Stay the night," Scott requested when Abby indicated it was about time to drive back to Kolton Lake.

"Are you sure about that?" She gave him a tentative look as they lay in bed, where he was massaging her feet. "Wouldn't want to overstay my welcome."

"You wouldn't be doing that," he told her, surprised she would assume otherwise. "It's late and I want you around so I can make my famous cinnamon pancakes with maple syrup for you in the morning." He scrunched up his face. "Pretty please."

"Well, when you put it that way." She giggled, brushing up against him. "I do like pancakes and maple syrup."

"Then it's settled." Scott grinned and continued to massage her soft toes and heels. "How does that feel?"

"So good." Abby shut her eyes. "Mmm."

He kept it going, happy to pleasure her in any and every way he could. "I can think of a few other things that might feel even better," he teased her.

"Oh, really?" Her lashes fluttered coquettishly. "Let me guess…"

He chuckled. "Don't try too hard."

The natural banter between them left an impression on Scott, making him believe that what they had was more than just sexual chemistry and physical attraction. He could tell that she felt the same way, even if she was being as careful as he was for fear of having her heart broken. Giving in to their carnal instincts, though, led to them making love again.

Only, this time, it was slow and deliberate, with Scott wanting to explore every part of Abby, and allowing her the same courtesy toward him, as they made love well into the wee hours of the morning. Afterward, they cuddled and whispered a few sweet words to one another before falling asleep on a very good note.

IN THE MORNING, Scott allowed Abby to get some extra shut-eye, while he checked his messages on the laptop for any news pertaining to the investigation. He got word that the FBI Laboratory was still working diligently to see if any of the retesting of forensic evidence related to

Veronica Liu's murder yielded any positive results. He would follow up on it later.

Right now, he needed to prepare the breakfast he'd promised Abby before she awakened. Seeing her sleeping so peacefully like an angel stirred him, making Scott imagine it could become a regular thing after a night of making love. He, for one, wanted to experience again the sense of a real commitment in companionship and beyond. Whether or not Abby was of the same mind was something that would need to be determined, sooner or later.

Scott had just poured the pancake batter on the electric griddle, with the bacon already made, when Abby walked into the kitchen in her bare feet. She was wearing one of his oversize plaid shirts and it looked sexy on her. "Good morning, sleepyhead," he told her.

"Morning." She ran a hand through her hair haphazardly. "Smells good."

"It'll taste even better." He grinned. "Coffee's ready. Help yourself."

"Thanks." Abby grabbed a mug out of the cabinet and poured coffee into it. "So, is there anything you can't do well?"

Scott laughed, though he wasn't sure if she was referring to in bed or in the kitchen. Or even as a cold case detective. "I'm sure I can think of a few things," he voiced honestly. "But I'll take the compliment anyhow."

"You should." She colored. "What can I say, Mr. Lynley, you know how to treat a woman well, in more ways than one."

"Back at you, Ms. Zhang," Scott told her sincerely while reading between the lines and liking the progress of the book. He tossed pancakes on a platter with the bacon and said, "Breakfast is served."

She beamed. "Perfect."

An hour later, Scott gave Abby a kiss good-bye and watched as she got into her car and drove home. Though barely out of his grasp, he was already starting to miss her and wondered when they might get to do a repeat of the overnight stay. Hell, he was even willing to go further and admit that the feelings he was developing for the victim specialist were much stronger than seeing Abby whenever time allowed in their schedules. But this needed to be kept in check. At least while giving her the space she needed to make her own assessment of where they were and could be headed.

He went to the barn to tend to the horses and clean the stalls. When he got back to the house, Scott's eyes lit up when he received a call from his sister Annette. A few months younger than his brother, Russell, she had been adopted as an infant by their parents, completing the Lynley family.

He flopped onto the retro upholstered armchair in the great room and accepted the video request. "Hey, there," he said after her face appeared on the small screen.

"Hello, Scott." Annette was biracial and attractive with bold brown-green eyes and long, wavy brunette hair with a middle part and chinlength bangs. A detective with the Dabs County Sheriff's Department, based in Carol Creek, Indiana, Annette was married to Indiana State Police Organized Crime and Corruption Unit Investigator Hamilton McCade.

"Was just thinking about you," Scott had to admit, more or less, as the image of Abby wearing her cowgirl hat entered his head.

"Really?" Annette chuckled. "Hope the thoughts were pleasant."

"Always." He grinned. "Actually, your name came up yesterday when I lent someone the riding hat you left behind. I figured you wouldn't mind."

"Of course not. The bigger question is, who is the special lady you invited to the ranch to go riding?" She gave him the inquiring eye.

"Her name is Abby Zhang. She's a victim specialist for the Bureau." Scott decided he might as well give his sister more of what she wanted. "We've hit it off."

"Seriously?" Annette batted her eyes. "That's wonderful to hear, Scott." Her teeth shone. "I'm so glad you finally decided to let someone in again."

"Me too," he admitted. Maybe if things went his way, this time he could succeed where he had previously failed. "We're still in the early stages, but it looks promising right now."

"Promising is a good place to start." Annette smiled. "Like the rest of us Lynleys, you deserve to be happy and in love. I know you probably aren't quite ready to use the L-word, but it's something to think about."

"I'm doing just that." Scott didn't want to get ahead of himself, though it was hard not to fall in love with someone like Abby. But before he allowed himself to go quite that far, he needed to know that the feelings were reciprocated and go from there. Switching subjects, Scott said, in noting that it was Annette who'd phoned him, "So, what's happening with you?"

"Oh, just the usual small-town crime." She chuckled frivolously. "And missing my favorite oldest sibling."

"Back at you." He grinned. "You and Hamilton are welcome to visit anytime you like."

"I can say the same to you, Scott. Even feel free to bring Abby along."

"Thanks. I'll keep that in mind." Scott hoped

Abby could meet his sisters and brother one day, as they would surely bond, as he had with their significant others. But only when she was ready and willing.

He told Annette a little about the cold case connection between Abby and the homicide victim from twenty years ago, Veronica Liu.

"Wow." Annette's brow puckered. "Sorry to hear about Abby's aunt."

"It was a long time ago."

"Never long enough when something like that happens."

"You're right," he conceded. "Abby's dealing with it as best as possible."

"Hope you catch the killer, if they're still around."

"That's the objective."

Shortly after the call ended, Scott received an ominous text message on his phone.

Drop the Veronica Liu investigation. Otherwise, her niece Abby is next. Unless you want her death on your conscience, move on to another cold case.

The stark warning sent a chill up and down Scott's spine as he got to his feet. Who sent him the text? Had it come from Veronica Liu's killer? Or was someone else messing with him for some reason?

Scott sucked in a deep breath and peeked out the window, as though expecting to see someone surveilling his property. He saw no one. It didn't make him any less concerned. Was Abby in danger? Or only if he continued to pursue the case? Should he warn her that she could be in danger? Or would such a warning only cause Abby to worry needlessly?

Scott began pacing. *Would I be playing with fire by putting a possible killer to the test in continuing to dig into the case?* he asked himself after again reading the threatening text message. He had begun to care for Abby too much to want to see her hurt. Much less killed, as her aunt Veronica had been.

But as an FBI special agent who was dedicated to the job and obligated to perform as required to the best of his ability, backing off a case was not an option. The way Scott saw it, someone was beginning to feel the heat insofar as the investigation into Veronica Liu's murder. That meant he was getting close to nailing the culprit, indicating the unsub was still alive and desperate to evade detection and apprehension. Making them all the more dangerous.

It makes me even more determined to close the books on this investigation with an arrest, Scott mused, taking a breath. But he was equally committed to ensuring Abby's safety, whatever it took. In this case, it had to start with warning her. Just in case this was more than an idle threat. He would also have the Bureau see if the text could be traced and sender identified.

ABBY HAD JUST finished taking a shower and changing clothes, when she got a call from Scott, who wanted a video chat. Fresh thoughts of their night of passion rolled through her mind, and what it might portend for the future, before she accepted the request. His handsome face appeared on the screen. "Hey." She kept her tone neutral, though admittedly having butterflies in their first communication since she'd driven away from his ranch a few hours ago.

"Hi. I see you made it back."

"Of course." She looked at him, trying to read his eyes. "Did you think I wouldn't?"

"Just glad to see that you did." He paused thoughtfully. "After you left, I got a weird text message."

"How weird?"

"Someone warned me to stop the investigation into your aunt's murder..." Scott began, "or put your life at risk."

"Seriously?" Abby's eyes widened with shock. "I'm being threatened now?"

"I'm afraid so." Scott's brow creased. "Looks as if the unsub believes it's only a matter of time now before the cloak of hiding in plain view for years comes crashing down. The killer is sending a clear message that threatening to come after you unless I back off will somehow do the trick."

"I'd never want you to give up finding my aunt Veronica's killer—" Abby made it clear "—by allowing our personal relationship to interfere with your job as a cold case investigator." She would never put such pressure on him in what would be a major conflict of interest. No matter the strength of her feelings for him. Or vice versa.

"I know." Scott seemed to read her mind. "I feel the same way. Giving in to intimidation would be a big mistake," he stressed.

"I agree."

"Could be the unsub is just bluffing. Or not. Either way, you need to watch your back, Abby."

"I will," she promised, and thought about carrying pepper spray and being aware of her surroundings.

"I'll try to see if I can track down the sender of the text message," Scott said and took a breath. "In the meantime, I wouldn't want anything bad to happen to you."

"Neither would I." Abby felt the strong vibes between them. The last thing she could imagine was having her life cut short like her aunt's and, in the process, ending whatever she seemed to be building with Scott. A thought suddenly occurred to Abby that seemed worth mentioning. "This may or may not mean anything, but a couple of days ago when I was at the hospital for work, I thought I saw Zach Gilliard at the end of the corridor. Only, when I tried to verify this, he was gone. Then when driving to see you yesterday, I thought an SUV was following me."

Scott's brows knitted. "Why didn't you tell me?"

"Because when the SUV continued on after I exited the highway, I figured it was all in my head," she asserted. "Not worth bringing up. Probably still was nothing. Or maybe Zach is stalking me but trying to do so at a safe distance. I don't know."

"You're right. The SUV may not have been tailing you." He paused. "Or didn't want you to think so." Scott rested for a moment on that disturbing possibility. "As for Gilliard, as long as he stays away from you and hasn't threatened you verbally or physically in any identifiable way, there's not much we can do at the moment but stay alert."

"Okay." Abby sucked in a calming breath. "I'll be careful. But don't stop trying to find my aunt's killer. She deserves the chance to rest in peace."

"You're right, she does," Scott concurred. "And you deserve some closure and to get on with your life."

"True." She wondered how much of that life he would be a part of once the investigation had reached its conclusion.

After they disconnected, Abby went over in her mind everything they had talked about. Whatever happened from this point on, she was determined not to live her life in fear. Wasn't that something she tried to instill as a victim specialist in others? Besides, having Scott and the Bureau itself on her side made Abby feel that she had nothing to worry about. Or at least those worries shouldn't overwhelm her. Not when she suddenly had renewed optimism for what the future might hold.

Chapter Eleven

On Monday, Abby was at work when she got a call from the mayor's office, asking if she could meet with Mayor Myerson this afternoon. Of course, Abby jumped on this, figuring that the woman might have something useful to add to the ongoing investigation into the murder of Veronica Liu. In spite of the mayor's previous contention that their relationship had been limited.

With the possibility that her aunt's killer was now targeting Abby, she recognized that the sooner the unsub was exposed and brought to justice, the better.

At 1:00 p.m. sharp, Abby showed up as scheduled and was led into the office of Freda Myerson. The mayor was on the phone but got off swiftly and pasted a smile on her face. "Abby." She stood up and rounded her desk, putting out a hand. "Nice to see you again."

Abby smiled. "You too."

"Thanks for coming in."

"Thanks for inviting me," Abby said, restraining her curiosity.

"Have a seat," Freda told her, then asked, "Would you like some coffee or tea?"

Abby declined. "No thanks, I'm good."

"Okay." The mayor sat beside her in a fabric lounge chair near the window. "I ran into Jeanne Singletary over the weekend," she noted, a twinkle in her aquamarine eyes.

"You did?" Abby had come to believe they did not run in the same circles.

"Yes. We hadn't seen each other in a while, but given the reopening of the case into Veronica's death, it seemed like a good time to catch up." Freda sat back and regarded her thoughtfully. "How's the investigation progressing?"

Abby mused about this and Scott's efforts in cracking the case, before responding, "From what I understand, Agent Lynley is still reviewing old evidence and reinterviewing suspects. Not sure just how much progress has been made." Abby was certain, though, that Scott had managed to touch a nerve of quite possibly the unsub. That meant that Scott may have been closer to nailing the perp than met the eye.

"I see." Freda rested her hands in her lap. "Well, I want you to know that as mayor of Kolton Lake, I stand by my promise to offer assistance in any way I can to help the Bureau and Agent Lynley in their efforts to solve this twenty-year-old mystery."

"I appreciate that, Mayor Myerson," Abby said sincerely.

"Anyway, your name came up when chatting with Jeanne," she said casually.

"Did it?"

"Yes." Freda grinned. "We were talking about your work with the FBI as a victim specialist and how much you've given of your life to help others who have also been traumatized in one way or another." She paused. "Anyway, I thought that another way for you to honor Veronica's memory would be to join my Crime Victims Advisory Board."

Abby lifted a brow. "Really?"

"Yes, I think you'd make a great addition to the board, helping victims of violence and criminality in Kolton Lake transition to becoming survivors and pushing beyond their victimization in bettering their lives." Freda reached out and touched Abby's arm. "So, what do you say? Is this something you would be interested in?"

"Of course." Abby didn't need to take long to consider it, knowing that extending her ability to assist other victims of violent crime was a no-brainer. She was certain that the Bureau would approve of this additional role for her. "I'd be honored to become a member of your Crime Victims Advisory Board, Mayor Myerson."

"Terrific." Freda flashed her teeth. "And please call me Freda. We're all like family here, even if we could never replace your wonderful aunt Veronica."

Abby nodded gratefully. "Thank you."

"No, thank you, Abby." Freda patted her hand. "I'd say this position is long overdue for you, as I'm sure my predecessor as mayor would attest to."

After leaving the mayor's office, Abby rang Scott to share the exciting news. "You'll never guess who I just met with?"

"Hmm…don't keep me in suspense."

"Mayor Myerson," she told him, standing outside and zeroing in on a pair of northern cardinals flying by. "Or Freda, as she now insists that I call her."

"Did she remember something pertinent about your aunt?"

"Actually, the mayor wants me to join her Crime Victims Advisory Board."

"Is that so?"

Abby chuckled. "Yes, I was surprised too. Of course, I accepted."

"As you should have." Scott spoke supportively. "You can certainly do some good in spreading your reach as a victim advocate."

"My sentiments precisely." She switched the phone to her other ear. "Anything yet on who sent the text message?"

"Not yet." His voice dropped. "I'm working on it. I'll let you know what I come up with, if anything."

"All right."

"Be careful," Scott reiterated.

"I will," she promised and they said goodbye.

Heading to her car, Abby glanced over her shoulder, almost for effect. But more to see if there might have been a stalker or decades-old killer on the prowl. There was no one. She couldn't help but wonder if this was the calm before the storm. Or was the threat to her life being overblown?

Her thoughts moved in a more positive direction toward a new position with the mayor's Crime Victims Advisory Board and the good Abby believed she could do beyond her role with the Bureau in helping those most in need.

SCOTT CERTAINLY WELCOMED Abby having a role with Mayor Myerson's advisory board in assisting victims in getting over the hump. She had earned the right to be herself and spread her wings as Abby continued to use her skills with the Bureau. He was happy to have her in his life, as well, and could see nothing but good things ahead for them. But right now, his chief concern was tracking down whoever had sent him that text, while threatening Abby in the process.

Trying to interfere in an FBI cold case investigation wasn't the smartest thing. Yet the unsub had chosen to do just that, indicating to Scott the sense of urgency or panic felt for stopping the investigation cold before the truth emerged.

Well, that isn't going to happen, he vowed to himself, driving from his office to the Kentucky Regional Computer Forensics Laboratory on North Whittington Parkway. Not as long as he was on the case. He had promised Abby that he wouldn't stop until a killer had been identified. He owed it to her to see this through for more reasons than one. Not the least of which was that he cared for her and didn't want to come up short in giving Abby the peace of mind that was twenty years in the making.

After arriving at his destination, Scott headed inside and met with Margaret Kanoho, a digital evidence examiner. A native Hawaiian, Margaret was in her late thirties, slender, with black hair in a cropped pixie.

"Hello, Scott." She gazed at him with expectant brown eyes. "What do you need?"

"I need to track an anonymous text message I received," he responded, knowing this was a given the moment he received the disturbing text.

"Okay. Let's see what we can do." He handed her his cell phone and watched as she read the text out loud. "'Drop the Veronica Liu investigation. Otherwise, her niece Abby is next. Unless you want her death on your conscience, move on to another cold case.'"

"Someone is trying to put the brakes on my current investigation," Scott pointed out.

"I can see that." Margaret made a face. "Why don't we head over to the cell phone investigative kiosk, extract the data we can pull from the text, and put the info in a report and make a copy of it for your computer? Shouldn't take much more than thirty minutes or so."

"Okay." He gave a nod. "Let's do it."

Less than an hour later, Margaret said, "Not too surprisingly, it looks like the text came from a burner phone. We can trace the approximate location from where it was sent and see what other clues we can access. But my guess is, if the unsub was smart, he or she probably ditched the cell phone, making it that much harder to track down. Or the user."

"Figured as much." Scott's brow furrowed. "Still, why don't you dig deeper and maybe we'll get lucky."

"You've got it." She rubbed her nose. "I'll need some time, but will do some further forensic analysis of the data and let you know if I come up with anything more definitive."

"Thanks."

"If the anonymous texter is emboldened enough, the unsub will keep at it and make a mistake that can lead you right to the culprit's door," Margaret suggested.

"If that happens, I'll be ready to pounce," Scott clearly confirmed.

He left the RCFL and headed back to his office to further examine the data collected and cross-reference it with the info he had on earlier suspects to see if it triggered anything.

At 6:00 P.M., feeling the need to unwind, Abby got together with her friend Beverly Welch at Kolton Lake Park for a run. Sitting on the shores of Lake Kolton, the well-worn wide path was bordered by hickory and oak trees. Abby shared the news of her recent undertaking as they meandered their way along, passing other runners.

"Seriously?" Beverly widened her brown eyes. "It's wonderful that Mayor Myerson asked you to be part of her Crime Victims Advisory Board."

"I know, right?" Abby grinned in agreement. "Seems like the perfect complement to my duties with the FBI."

"Yeah, that's true. Just be sure you don't overwork yourself, so you don't have time to hang with your friends."

Abby laughed. "I'll always find time to hang with you, Bev," she promised.

"You better." Beverly gave her a warning look. "With a rambunctious ten-year-old running me ragged at times, I need my adult space with friends to maintain my sanity."

"I understand." Abby considered the possibility of becoming a mother herself someday, longing to have one or two children to run after day and night. She somehow found that to be much more inviting than a chore.

"Good. So, Ms. Advisory Board Member, what do you say we pick up some speed here and see who can reach the lake first?"

"You're on." Abby accepted the challenge, even as Beverly dashed ahead of her, momentarily leaving her in the dust.

Just as Abby started to pick up the pace, she heard another runner quickly approaching from behind. She felt herself being shoved to the ground, hitting it hard. Dazed, Abby heard a gruff male voice say, "Tell Agent Lynley to back off. Final warning!"

As she digested this ominous warning with the sounds of her attacker leaving, Abby saw a hooded, tall figure race off into the trees. Having had the wind knocked out of her, she struggled to get to her feet.

She was still wobbly when Beverly ran up to her and asked perceptively, while helping her to remain upright, "What happened?"

"I—I was attacked," Abby stammered.

"By who?"

Abby asked herself the same question. Was it Zach Gilliard? Or the unsub who'd sent Scott the text message? Could they have inexplicably been one and the same?

She pointed toward the woods in the direction the assailant had sprinted off, as though expecting him to still be within view.

Beverly peered. "I don't see anyone."

"Neither do I," Abby admitted. The person who had attacked her had vanished from sight completely.

As soon as he heard that Abby had been assaulted by someone in the park, Scott practically broke the speed limit driving to Kolton Lake. All kinds of thoughts raced through his head. Was this the work of the unsub who'd texted him? It appeared to be so, not just some random attack in the park.

Scott replayed the attacker's alarming words to Abby.

Tell Agent Lynley to back off. Final warning!

The unsub had clearly taken the threats to a whole new level after the text, as though Scott hadn't gotten the message. And that had turned into a direct physical threat to Abby's life. Or, at the very least, the unsub's way of demonstrating just what he was capable of, with Abby sure that she had been assaulted by a male attacker.

The one thing Scott knew for certain was that he couldn't bear the thought of losing Abby to violence. Not when they both suddenly had a lot more to live for in developing a bond that still needed to be explored over the course of time.

When he pulled into Abby's driveway, Scott saw her familiar vehicle and a gray Genesis G70 sedan. Exiting his SUV, he ran up to the log cabin, and the door was opened by Abby herself.

"Are you okay?" Scott asked her inside, disregarding her reassurances over the phone to that effect.

"I'm fine," she reiterated, forcing a smile. "Just a few minor aches and pains from being thrown to the ground."

Scott noted that she was still in her jogging

attire and looked a little ruffled, but otherwise was not the worse for wear. He gazed at the other person standing in the room.

"This is my friend Beverly Welch," Abby told him. "She was running just ahead of me when the attack occurred."

He acknowledged her. "Hey, Beverly."

"Hi."

"Scott's an FBI agent," Abby told her. "He's the one who reopened the cold case into my aunt Veronica's murder."

Beverly cocked a brow musingly. "Do you think this has something to do with that?" she asked him.

"Undoubtedly." Scott pondered the stark intimidation tactic sent to both of them and turned to Abby. "Did you get a good look at the attacker?"

"I'm afraid not." She sucked in a deep breath.

"What can you tell me about him?" he pressed.

"Only that he was tall, wore a hoodie and darkish clothing. It all happened so fast." Abby wrung her hands as she met Scott's steady gaze.

He angled his face. "Did the voice have any degree of familiarity?"

"Not really." She started at the question. "He seemed to be trying to disguise his voice by speaking in a raspy tone."

That didn't surprise Scott. All in all, the unsub was clearly going the extra mile to hide his identity. But this could only go so far. "Maybe surveillance video can help us identify him," he suggested.

"Maybe." Abby twisted her lips musingly. "Not sure if it makes any sense, with respect to Aunt Veronica's death and your investigation, but I think it could have been Zach Gilliard who attacked me."

Scott chewed on that unsettling thought as he got on his cell phone and asked that Gilliard be immediately brought in for questioning.

Chapter Twelve

Scott sat in an armless stacking chair, across a small metal table from Zach Gilliard, in an interrogation room at the FBI's Owensboro satellite office. He studied the unemployed warehouse worker, who Scott had previously decided was likely not a stalker in the true sense of the word for Abby to be concerned with. Had he misjudged Gilliard? Was he missing something about the man that could have linked him to the murder of Veronica Liu?

At forty-three, Zach Gilliard would have been twenty-three when Abby's aunt had been killed. That was certainly old enough for him to have targeted her. If so, why? And how had he managed to avoid a criminal record void of violence? Or other acts of aggression?

As though he hadn't a clue, Gilliard narrowed his eyes and asked, "Mind telling me what I'm doing here?"

Scott jutted his chin and snapped straightforwardly, "Two hours ago, Abby Zhang was attacked in Kolton Lake Park. Know anything about that?"

"Abby?" Gilliard wrinkled his forehead. "The victim specialist?"

"I think you know who she is," Scott said tartly. "Answer the question."

"I have no idea what you're talking about," he claimed. "I'm sorry someone attacked Abby. I hope she wasn't hurt badly, but I had nothing to do with it."

Scott peered at him. "Where were you at that time?"

"I was at work," the suspect said matter-of-factly.

Scott was dubious. "And where is work exactly?"

"Octalinn Industries, here in Owensboro, on East Second Street," he answered calmly. "I was hired two days ago as a forklift operator. Worked till 7:30 p.m. You can check with my supervisor, Genevieve Plunkett."

"I'll do that," Scott told him, making a note. He stared at him for a long moment, then asked curiously, "Did you live in the area twenty years ago?"

Gilliard leaned back, pensive. "Twenty years ago, I was living in New York City," he claimed. "Why do you ask?"

Scott ignored the question while thinking that should be easy enough to verify. "Does the name Veronica Liu mean anything to you?"

"No," Gilliard responded without preface. "Why should it?"

"No reason." Scott stood. "Hold tight for just a few minutes."

When he returned to the interrogation room, it was with the knowledge that Gilliard's alibi did check out. He wasn't the one who had attacked Abby. Scott could understand how she may have made that assumption, given Gilliard's penchant for apparently hanging around where he wasn't wanted. Not to mention the heat of the moment in not seeing the unsub's face, but in determining he was apparently of similar size. Hell, even the clothing Gilliard was wearing was not unlike what Abby had described of the attacker.

Yet Zach Gilliard clearly isn't our culprit. Scott eyed him at the table. "Your alibi held up."

Gilliard flashed a triumphant expression. "Am I free to go?"

"Just about." While he had the man's attention, Scott figured he may as well get some mileage out of this. Especially when considering that Gilliard may have still been stalking Abby after she'd thought she'd seen him lurking around at the hospital. Scott leaned forward and told him in no uncertain tone, "Stay away from Abby Zhang. I get that she helped you deal with an uncomfortable situation. That's her job. But now you need to leave Ms. Zhang alone. Am I making myself clear?"

"Yeah." Gilliard lowered his chin. "Don't worry. I won't be bothering Abby anymore."

"Good."

Scott sighed, sure he received the intended message, loud and clear. He gave Gilliard permission to leave, feeling that with the understanding between them where Abby was concerned, it was one less headache to deal with. But there was still the attack on Abby. With Gilliard no longer a suspect, it meant that the unsub was still on the loose and doing whatever he could to impede the cold case investigation. Meaning that Abby was still a target for as long as the case was active.

THAT NIGHT, Abby was still a little shaken at the thought of someone attacking her at Kolton Lake Park. All in a brazen attempt to dissuade Scott from getting to the bottom of her aunt Veronica's death. The fact that it wasn't Zach Gilliard was somewhat of a relief. Having someone you only wanted to help become dangerously fixated on you was nothing any victim specialist would wish for. But at least Zach was a known entity that could have been dealt with accordingly.

Not so much for an unsub she couldn't identify. *If only I'd been able to get a better look at him*, Abby told herself, feeling restless lying beside Scott, who was sound asleep. But then again, the attacker's intent had obviously been to rattle her while camouflaging his identity. Meaning Scott would need more time to unravel the mystery, even while being quite understandably concerned for her safety. As she was. This notwithstanding, though, she wouldn't be bullied into asking him to back off the case and leave her aunt Veronica in limbo for another two decades.

No, if someone wished to come after her, Abby intended to do her best to ward off an attacker. At least to slow him down enough for the cavalry to come to the rescue. In this instance, very likely, in the form of Scott Lynley. His interest in her had clearly moved beyond an intimate connection. Or her being a gateway to the murder of her aunt Veronica. As had Abby's interest in the FBI special agent risen a few notches of late. Just how far they could climb this mountain played on her mind. And, if the truth be told, her heart, which was skipping beats more and more as it related to her growing affections for Scott.

Abby fell asleep in his arms while wishing the aunt she had lost twenty years ago was still around to be there as Abby worked toward her own future.

"HAVE YOU EVER been hypnotized?" Scott asked Abby the next morning as they sat across from one another in a booth at the Kolton Lake Breakfast House on Larameer Lane. After the attack on her yesterday, he found himself wanting to stay by Abby's side 24/7. Yet he knew that was neither practical nor achievable, no matter his concern for her safety, given that they both had jobs that demanded their attention. Not to mention, he doubted that Abby would agree to his being her bodyguard, coming at the expense of the investigation into her aunt's murder. Right now, Scott believed that the best thing he could do for Abby was double down and solve the two-decades-old homicide. And not allow a current unsub, and presumably Veronica Liu's killer, to derail him. But to do that, Scott knew he would need Abby's help in a way neither had anticipated with, admittedly, an unpredictable outcome.

"Hypnotized?" Abby's eyes grew as she gripped her mug of coffee. "No. I'm not even sure I subscribe to the notion of hypnotizing, per se." She gazed at him inquiringly. "Why do you ask?"

Scott sat back. "Well, I was thinking that it might be a good idea if you were to see a forensic psychologist the Bureau works with. She specializes in hypnosis," he told her, glancing at his ham and cheese omelet. "And yes, it does work, when done by a qualified professional. In this instance, it could help you recall more details about the person—or animal—you saw moving quickly through the woods."

Abby pursed her lips. "You really think I could remember something that I never truly was able to home in on that day?" she questioned, and tasted the coffee.

"You'd be surprised what we can retain in our day-to-day encounters, observations, experiences and the like," he told her. "Most times, it's irrelevant. Other times, though, it could be critical to uncovering evidence of a crime, details on an unsub and more. Many skilled forensic psychologists have been successful over the years in pulling out such hidden memories from a subject's subconscious. I think it may be worth taking a shot here to see if it reveals anything useful to the investigation. No matter how small. Moreover, I'm sensing that whoever killed Veronica Liu is likely the same unsub who attacked you and is feeling very threatened by the investigation and being exposed. This could be a way to bridge the twenty-year gap and get the jump on the unsub before he can try to come after you again."

"You're right," Abby allowed, and bit into a piece of avocado toast. "I want this to be over. If you believe hypnosis might bring us closer to the truth, then I'm in."

Scott gave a pleased nod. "Good. I'll set it up." He sliced his fork into the omelet. "Whatever happens, I'll be there for support."

She smiled. "I was counting on that."

He grinned back and knew instinctively that, no matter what, he intended to be there for her beyond the case that had brought them together. As far as he was concerned, Abby was a keeper, and so was he for the right person, believing she was that for him.

ABBY WAS ADMITTEDLY a little nervous about the notion of being put under by a psychologist, hypnotist or whatever. Even if she was somewhat skeptical of the whole process, she had actually read about hypnotherapy and some people who were apparently successfully hypnotized for everything from weight loss to trying to stop smoking. And yes, for unlocking repressed memories from childhood traumas. But in her case, she wasn't holding on to things too painful to remember. In her mind, the memories of that tragic day were still pretty clear. Whatever she'd seen in the woods was not something she was hiding from, like a boogeyman. But rather something that had caught her eye at a cursory glance. She'd never pinned it to memory beyond the vague image that whizzed by.

Or had she locked away something that a forensic psychologist could indeed bring to the surface? And, in the process, help Scott nail a killer still on the prowl?

When they entered the Rutherford Building on East Main Street in downtown Louisville that afternoon, Abby had calmed her nerves, deciding she would be a big girl in continuing to do what she could to recall anything that could provide clues in the cruel murder of her aunt Veronica. If all else failed, it was surely another bonding experience of sorts with Scott.

On the fifth floor, they got off the elevator and stood outside the door of Dr. Rosalind Jimenez, a licensed clinical psychologist.

Scott took Abby's hands, steadying her as he said comfortingly, "You'll be fine."

She nodded and took a breath. "Let's do this."

Inside the office, they were greeted by a petite and slender Latina in her early forties, with brown eyes and blond hair in a shoulder-length cut and choppy bangs. She was stylishly dressed in an ivory skirt suit and designer sandals.

"I'm Dr. Jimenez," she introduced herself to Abby.

She shook the psychologist's hand. "Abby Zhang."

Rosalind faced Scott. "Nice to see you again, Agent Lynley."

"You too." He gave her a thin smile. "Thanks for seeing us on short notice."

"Happy to fit you in," she said, eyeing Abby. "I hope I can help you discover something long-buried that may be beneficial to Agent Lynley's investigation."

"Me too," Abby told her.

After Scott had settled in a separate viewing room to watch the session on a video screen, with Abby's permission, she went with Dr. Jimenez to the therapy room, noting that it looked more like a living room setting with its contemporary furnishings and native plants strategically placed to, Abby assumed, help patients feel relaxed.

After a brief explanation for how this worked, Abby lay on a quilted recliner chair, while the doctor took a seat nearby in an upholstered wingback chair.

It seemed to take only moments before Abby

was in a relaxed state and found herself in a trip back in time to when she was twelve years old.

"Tell me what happened when you first got off the school bus," Rosalind said.

Abby took a breath and uttered, "I waved goodbye to my friends and walked to my aunt Veronica's log cabin, a block away."

"Did you see anyone else at that point?"

"No."

"What happened then?" the psychologist asked.

"I saw Aunt Veronica's car in the driveway," Abby responded. "I could see that she was inside."

"What did you do then?"

"I walked over to the car and... I saw her sitting motionless behind the steering wheel." Abby sucked in a deep breath. "There was blood on my aunt's face," she cried. "Lots of it."

Rosalind said to her in a gentle tone, "I know that's difficult to see, Abby, so let's move on. Turn away from your aunt and look toward the woods." She paused. "Are you doing that?"

"Yes." Abby focused on the wooded area. "I see the trees."

"What else do you see in the woods, Abby?" she asked. "Is there someone out there? Take your time..."

Studying the woods, Abby sighed and replied, "There is something out there. Moving fast."

"It is a human or animal?" the psychologist asked.

"Human," she answered positively.

"Can you tell if the person is a man or woman?"

Abby peered through the deep recesses of her mind while zeroing in as best she could on the subject. "Looks like a man," she uttered, her voice lifted an octave.

"What can you tell me about him?" Rosalind pressed.

"Can't see much of him through the trees." Abby strained to gather more information. "Tall and... I think he might have glanced back at me..." Her voice shook. "I think he may have killed Aunt Veronica—"

"Try not to think about that part," the psychologist stressed evenly. "Concentrate again on this man and see if you can describe anything he's wearing."

"Dark pants," Abby said after a moment or two, then added, "He's got on a bright red windbreaker with the hood over his head." She made a strange sound. "He's gone now. Can't see him anymore."

"That's fine," Rosalind told her. "I'm going to bring you out of this and back to the present."

"Okay." Abby heard numbers being counted backward and it seemed as though she was passing through a time machine of sorts before suddenly opening her eyes. She was slightly disoriented, momentarily, as she sat up, while focusing on the forensic psychologist. "How did I do?"

Rosalind's eyes crinkled at the corners. "You did good, Abby. I think the memories we unlocked may prove useful to Agent Lynley."

"Really?" Abby could only vaguely recall what she'd seen and said.

"Yeah, you've given us more to work with in the investigation," Scott said matter-of-factly after walking into the room. He glanced at Rosalind. "Thanks for helping Abby to see some critical details of her experience that got lost in the corridors of time."

"It was my pleasure," she told him coolly. "Not to mention, my job as a clinical psychologist. Hope you're able to solve the case you're working on."

"And that's my job," he responded with confidence in his inflection. "We'll get it done."

Abby watched him as Scott met her eyes warmly and seemed to indicate that there was, indeed, light at the end of the tunnel that they both would soon be able to bask in.

Chapter Thirteen

"Call it a hunch," Scott told Abby as they headed back to Kolton Lake after the hypnosis session with Dr. Rosalind Jimenez. "The fact that while under hypnosis you felt you did see an adult male running through the woods and he appeared to have seen you, tells me that the unsub may see you as not simply a means to get me to drop the investigation by bloodline, but as a direct threat to identifying him."

"Seriously?" Abby shifted in the passenger seat. "But I didn't truly see his face in a way where I could point him out in a lineup or anything."

"But he doesn't know that," Scott surmised from behind the wheel. "Yes, the distance between you at the time would make such an identification highly unlikely. However, the unsub may feel he can't afford to take that chance. Hence the threats and attack on you, as we draw nearer to fingering him, one way or another."

"So, how will we go about doing that?" she queried. "The unsub still seems to be holding some of the key cards, at least in terms of getting to him and making an arrest."

"Well, I'm not much of a card player," Scott quipped, "but I'm more than capable of playing the hand I've been dealt. In this case, clothing you believe the unsub was wearing could provide some important clues about him."

"Such as?"

"Such as if the unsub did have on a bright red windbreaker, something that stands out, it's possible someone may remember a person with such a jacket."

Abby blinked. "I suppose."

Scott sat back. "Based on the nature of the attack, with robbery being ruled out more or less, my guess is that the unsub knew your aunt. Either on a personal level or work-related. In both cases, one person may be best positioned to speak to this, in terms of the red jacket he wore."

"Who?" Abby eyed him curiously.

"Your aunt's best friend and business partner," Scott said, ruminating. "Jeanne Singletary."

ABBY WAS ADMITTEDLY piqued as she and Scott drove to Singletary Realty. It seemed like a long shot at best that Jeanne would remember two decades later what she'd even worn back then on a given day. *Much less someone who knew my aunt Veronica*, Abby thought pessimistically. But there was always the possibility. She was open to anything that might assist Scott in breaking the case. As it was, Abby was still coming to grips with memories she'd never known were there being brought to the surface. She had seen someone, who had apparently seen her. And was willing to do whatever it took to silence her, while keeping her aunt's murder mystery just that.

When they entered the office, Jeanne was standing, holding a mug of coffee. She smiled. "Abby." And gazed through her glasses at Scott. "Agent Lynley."

Abby accepted her hug. "Hi, Jeanne."

After Scott acknowledged her, Jeanne eyed Abby and said, "I understand that you've accepted a role with Freda Myerson's Crime Victims Advisory Board."

"I have," she told her, remembering that the mayor had spoken with Jeanne before making the offer. "Seems like a good thing."

Jeanne grinned. "I couldn't agree more. You'll make a great asset to the board and I know that Veronica would approve."

"I think so too," Abby agreed maudlinly.

Jeanne shifted her eyes from one to the other

before landing solidly on Scott, and asked, "Do you have news on the investigation?"

"Yes," he responded equably. "Yesterday, someone attacked Abby at Kolton Lake Park."

"What?" Jeanne's brow wrinkled. She turned to Abby. "Were you hurt?"

"No," she told her. "Just a couple of bruises, and I had the wind knocked out of me."

"And you think this had something to do with your case?" Jeanne asked Scott.

"Yes. I was warned to close the case or Abby would be next." He spoke bluntly. "Then, in apparently following through on this, someone came after her in the park. Unfortunately, Abby didn't get a clear look at the attacker."

"I'm so glad you weren't seriously injured," Jeanne told her. "The fact that this person would go after your aunt and continue this pattern of violence against you twenty years later is sickening."

"Tell me about it." Abby wrinkled her nose. "We need to stop this."

Jeanne nodded. "I agree." Her cell phone rang but she ignored it. "Is there anything I can do to help?"

Scott lowered his chin and said, "As a matter of fact, there may be." He paused. "Abby went under hypnosis to see if she could remember anything relevant the day Veronica Liu was murdered."

"Really?" Jeanne put a hand on Abby's shoulder. "Did this trigger any memories?"

Abby waited a beat and answered unevenly, "I remembered there was a man running off into the woods, presumably away from the car where Aunt Veronica lay mortally wounded."

Jeanne's lower lip hung in shock. "Can you identify him?"

"No, he was too far away," Abby replied, disappointed that her twelve-year-old self had not been closer and more fixated on the man in the woods.

"What she did remember was that the unsub was wearing a bright red hooded windbreaker," Scott said. "I know it's been years, but do you happen to recall anyone in Veronica Liu's professional or social circles who may have worn such a jacket at that time?"

"Actually, I think I do." She pushed her glasses up pensively. "Oliver Dillman had a jacket matching that very description."

Scott glanced at Abby. "Your former employee?"

"Yes, that's the one," Jeanne stated. "I remember thinking that it stood out. I told him once, and he just brushed it off." She sighed. "Or maybe not. It seemed like, at one point, he did stop wearing the jacket. Come to think of it, it may have been after Veronica was killed."

Abby caught Scott's gaze, prompting her to say, "Maybe there was some symmetry there." She tried to picture if the shadowy male figure she'd seen in the woods that day two decades ago was, in fact, Oliver Dillman. Or, for that matter, the man who'd attacked her a day ago. She couldn't positively identify him for either crime. But the pieces did seem to fit. "If Oliver did kill Aunt Veronica while wearing that red jacket, it would stand to reason that he'd want to get rid of it as evidence in a crime, along with the murder weapon."

"I was thinking the same thing," Scott told her.

"That bastard." Jeanne squinted her eyes. "I sensed he was trouble way back when. But didn't have anything to go on that would hold up."

"It's not your fault." Abby made it clear, knowing that she had voiced her suspicions back then. If guilty, the man had pulled the wool over everyone's eyes, including law enforcement. "We can only speculate at this point."

"It may be a little more than speculation," Scott said contemplatively.

"So, are you going to arrest him?" Jeanne asked anxiously, hand firmly on her hip.

"Afraid it's not quite that simple," he responded, pursing his lips. "To make an arrest that sticks, we'll need more than a distant memory of a bright red hooded jacket that Dillman has long gotten rid of to nail him, if he's the unsub." Scott exhaled. "But it is an important step in the right direction."

In Abby's mind, that step would have to do till they were sure that Oliver Dillman was responsible for her aunt Veronica's murder. Until such time, she needed to be on guard and let the Bureau do its job with Scott in full pursuit of justice.

THE FOLLOWING DAY, Scott was in his office. He had just gotten off the phone with Elodie Zimbalist, the FBI agent he had assigned to Abby's protection while her life was being threatened in connection with the Veronica Liu cold case investigation. Believing that the two women could actually end up as friends, Scott was confident that Agent Zimbalist, a fifteen-year veteran of the Bureau and wife of a federal air marshal, would keep Abby safe with a killer at large.

Scott now believed the unsub could well be, after all, Oliver Dillman, the fifty-eight-year-old real estate agent who'd been spurned by Veronica twenty years ago and apparently hadn't taken it very well. It made Scott wonder how he'd misread the man previously, if true. At least the timing and circumstantial evidence seemed to fit. Not to mention, the vague description of the unsub who'd attacked Abby could have been Dillman. But the fact remained that he had an alibi for Veronica Liu's death and had been dismissed by the original investigators on the case as a strong suspect, if one at all.

Had they missed a crucial clue in the red windbreaker? Or in the nature and potential of stalker violence? Had Dillman been tested for gunshot residue? Could he have had the time to go to the cabin then successfully get far enough away from it to convince the authorities that he couldn't have been in two places at once?

Scott went to his laptop for an update on the forensic evidence in the Veronica Liu murder being retested by the FBI Laboratory. The hope was that their efforts might yield results that could tie the cold case to Oliver Dillman. Or provide a legal justification for compelling him to submit DNA and fingerprints as potential evidence in a homicide.

Appearing on the screen for a video chat was Madeline McAuliffe. The thirtysomething forensic firearms analyst had dark hair in a short shag and blue eyes. She gave him a nod. "Agent Lynley."

"Hello." He got right to it. "Have you come up with anything on the .38 Special used in the killing of Veronica Liu?" he asked succinctly.

"Yes and no," Madeline said, running a hand through her hair. "As you know, the cartridge removed from the victim and the casing found at the crime scene were a match. Regarding the ammo itself, further testing showed this was fired from a gun barrel with four lands and grooves and had a right-hand twist." She paused. "We reentered the evidence of the cartridge casing into the NIBIN's identification system but, thus far, haven't come back with a hit."

"Okay." Scott wasn't particularly surprised with this, given the length of time that had passed since the homicide. Still, he'd held out hope that the murder weapon was still around. "What about the Colt Python .357 Magnum revolver used to commit the crime?"

"Nothing there." Madeline frowned. "The database has drawn a blank on the firearm being used in any other shootings. But hey, it's not out of the realm of possibility that the murder weapon will eventually show up and we can use the ATF's National Tracing Center to get all the info we can in tracing it to the unsub."

"Yeah." Scott went with that, knowing that time wasn't on their side in terms of getting some solid evidence that could tie Oliver Dillman to the heartless murder of Veronica Liu, before he got desperate enough to take another crack at Abby. Even in the capable hands of Agent Zimbalist, Scott did not wish to leave Dillman's possible deadly intentions to chance, if he could help it.

ELODIE ZIMBALIST WAS attractive and in her early thirties, like Abby. She regarded the slender, blue-eyed FBI agent, who had midlength sandy hair with a middle part, as they sat across the table from each other for lunch at Cheryl's Café on Frederica Street, near Smothers Park and Abby's office in Owensboro. When Scott had told her she would be given a bodyguard, Abby hadn't balked at the idea. If Oliver Dillman truly was out to get her as someone who he thought could identify him as her aunt Veronica's killer, Abby wasn't about to refuse protection and unnecessarily place herself in the line of fire.

On the contrary, she welcomed having the FBI agent shadowing her every move, making sure Abby didn't fall prey to the worries of a man who may have felt he had nothing to lose and everything to gain in seeing her dead. Besides that, Elodie, who had insisted she be called by her first name, seemed affable enough to Abby. She'd learned, in fact, that she and the agent had both graduated from the University of Kentucky and were both lifelong fans of the Kentucky Wildcats football team.

Abby found herself envious that Elodie was happily married, knowing matrimony was something she had yet to experience. Maybe this would forever elude her. Or maybe Scott was the husband material she thought him to be. She was willing to wait him out, if this was truly the direction they were headed.

"So, what's it like to work for the Bureau as a victim specialist?" Elodie broke her reverie while holding a cheesesteak sandwich. "As an agent, I see cases more from a law enforcement perspective."

Abby suspected that this was more casual conversation than anything, but was happy to engage. "Oh, it's often challenging and puts me in various scenarios where victims need immediate assistance, to one degree or another." She nibbled on her tuna sandwich. "Definitely keeps me on my toes."

Elodie smiled. "I'll bet."

"What about you?" Abby asked, dabbing a napkin to her lips. "I take it that security detail isn't your usual assignment?"

"No, it isn't." She laughed. "It is required from time to time, such as now, when someone involved in a federal investigation is a potential target. Mostly, though, I'm involved with gathering intel, making arrests, executing search warrants and, of course, the dreaded paperwork."

"Oh, yes." Abby chuckled. "I can certainly relate to the paperwork drudgery."

Both laughed again and Abby found herself even more relaxed with Elodie Zimbalist, in spite of knowing they'd been brought together because of a cold case that was suddenly beginning to heat up in ways that threatened to blow it wide open.

With Abby caught directly in the center of it.

Chapter Fourteen

That afternoon, Scott turned his attention to the scientific reanalysis of the latent print and DNA evidence found at the crime scene, in and outside of Veronica's Liu's Mercedes-Benz the day she was murdered. With the advances in forensic technology over the past two decades, he hoped they might be able to shed new light on an old crime. He was on a Skype three-way video call with the FBI crime lab's Latent Print Unit's forensic examiner Matt D'Angelo and the Federal DNA Database Unit's laboratory scientist Kay Nakata.

Scott gazed at D'Angelo, who was in his thirties, with dark hair in a pompadour cut, a corporate beard and gray eyes, and said to him, "Anything on the partial print?"

"Yeah, got something for you," he responded. "Using our advanced chemical processing methods and state-of-the-art equipment, we were able to conduct friction ridge analysis on the latent print to determine that it belongs to the unidentified person's left index finger. An important clue when trying to nail the perp."

Scott concurred, which begged the next question. "Were you able to come up with anything from the Next Generation Identification system?" he asked, referring to the FBI's fingerprint database.

D'Angelo scratched his beard. "Well, we've compared the latent print to millions of known prints identifiable in the system's holdings. Unfortunately, we have yet to get a hit. Afraid your unsub may have managed to lay low in avoiding arrest and the taking of finger and palm prints that could be matched with the latent fingerprint."

"Yeah, appears that way." Scott made a face when pondering his current top person of interest. He turned his attention to lab tech Kay Nakata. She, too, was in her thirties, and narrow-faced, with long frizzy brunette hair and hazel eyes. "How are we looking with the unidentified DNA profile?"

Kay smiled when she replied, "We can now confirm that, when retested, the DNA submission is definitely that of an unidentified male DNA profile."

Scott nodded to that effect, which could mean that it belonged to the unsub. Or, in this instance, the one he did now suspect of having perpetrated the murder.

Oliver Dillman.

"I don't suppose you were able to get a hit on the DNA profile through the national DNA index system?" Scott asked her, regarding this arm of the Bureau's Combined DNA Index System.

Kay lost the smile and responded wanly, "Wish I had good news on that front. Thus far, there are no hits on CODIS's arrestee or convicted offender indices or forensic index. As Matt indicated, seems as though your unsub has kept his nose clean for years, or has gone underground. Thereby circumventing the system to his benefit."

Scott bristled at the notion. "Now that I've reopened the case, I have a strong suspicion that the unsub has resurfaced and may be targeting a witness, Abby Zhang." *Who has become so much more to me*, he thought honestly. "I just need to connect the dots and see if they can stick."

"We'll keep pushing to try and make this happen, Agent Lynley," Matt told him.

"Thanks, Matt." Scott sat back. "I'll take what I can get."

Kay leaned forward. "You know, it may or may not be a long shot, but in coming up empty with CODIS, you could try going the investigative genetic genealogy route in trying to track down the unsub behind the unidentified DNA profile."

"I'm way ahead of you there, Kay." Scott lifted his chin musingly. "I've already reached out to KentuckyFam, the nonprofit Lexington-based genetic genealogy database service, to try and see if they can assist in this investigation, even while you continue to find matches."

Kay smiled. "Smart thinking. If they can make a connection at all, KentuckyFam will provide some leads that may yield some positive results. In the meantime, as you say, we'll stick to what we're doing, and maybe hit the jackpot."

"Okay," Scott said and ended the three-way conversation. He sat back in his desk chair and contemplated working with the genetic genealogy firm in seeking answers. Having gone down this road before, the results had been mixed. But all things considered, using KentuckyFam, a take on the Kentucky ancestral family tree, was a worthwhile avenue to pin down a killer who was still on the prowl. And apparently going after Abby to keep his deadly secret.

Though Scott wanted nothing more than to haul in Oliver Dillman, if for no other reason than as a suspect in the attack on Abby, doing so prematurely might jeopardize the possible case against the man for the murder of Veronica Liu. The last thing Scott needed was to spook Dillman into skipping town. Or to have the case fall apart due to lack of evidence. Thereby risking it remaining a cold case forever.

What would that do to my growing relationship with Abby, if this was to hang over us like a cumulus cloud? Scott couldn't help but wonder as he rose. He wanted them to work. Maybe more than anything he'd wanted in recent memory. But he didn't want to see Abby left hanging, with her beloved aunt's murder investigation still unfinished business. Not if he could do something about it that would be good for both of them.

CYNTHIA SALAZAR, a forensic genetic genealogist with KentuckyFam, relished the opportunity to work with the FBI in tackling the cold case homicide involving the death of thirty-one-year-old Veronica Liu. She understood that two decades had gone by since the homicide and most other efforts to track down the perpetrator had fallen short. But this was what KentuckyFam excelled at. Having been fairly successful with investigative genetic genealogy in criminal forensic investigations over the years, Cynthia truly believed they could lend a helping hand to the case.

The twenty-nine-year-old single mother-to-be sat in a midback-padded chair with armrests at her ergonomic desk, pondering the opportunistic task before her. According to FBI Special Agent Scott Lynley, his chief suspect in the murder of Veronica Liu was a fifty-eight-year-old man named Oliver Dillman. Problem was, in spite of irrefutable and indirect evidence tying him to the victim in one manner or another, Dillman's DNA was not in the CODIS database. Meaning that it could not be matched with the unidentified male profile found at the crime scene.

This was where Cynthia and Kentucky-Fam came in. Through genome sequencing, they could develop a genealogical profile from the DNA of the unknown male by analyzing identity-by-descent, matching DNA segments to show shared ancestries. With millions of genetic profiles that were readily accessible through genealogy databases, in her way of thinking, in combing through the genetic branches of the family tree, she stood a good chance of finding distant relatives of the unsub. This could go a long way in helping Agent Lynley to zoom in on his person of interest in the murder, especially when combined with demographic identifiers related to the chief suspect.

Now was the time to put her skills to the test, Cynthia believed. If the unidentified crime scene male DNA profile belonged to Oliver Dillman, she would need to give the Bureau a major reason to pursue this angle in the investigation. The rest would be up to the handsome special agent working the case.

THAT EVENING, Abby agreed to an overnight stay at Scott's ranch, with the cold case investigator temporarily relieving Agent Zimbalist of her duties. Though Abby enjoyed Elodie's company and saw her as a new friend, she welcomed spending more time with Scott. In spite of the tension in the air now that they appeared to be closing in on her aunt Veronica's killer but had yet to make the case against Oliver Dillman official.

After ordering Chinese takeout of moo goo gai pan and egg drop soup, they ate in the dining room.

Sitting across the solid wood trestle dining table from Scott in a cross-back side chair, Abby gazed at him and asked curiously, "Do you really think that forensic genetic genealogy might be the key to solving the murder of my aunt Veronica?"

"Perhaps." He forked some food. "Not a perfect science, but it's worked in the past to solve a number of big cold cases. If we can tie the DNA evidence from the crime scene to Oliver Dillman's familial line of DNA, we can compel Dillman to submit his own DNA for comparison with the unidentified male DNA profile. Especially given the work connection between Dillman and your aunt and her rejecting his advances, to go along with his owning at the time a red jacket much like the one you saw a man wearing while under hypnosis. Dillman also fit the general physical description of the man who attacked you at the park."

"That does make for a compelling argument," Abby had to admit as she spooned her soup and pictured Oliver Dillman, whom she recalled seeing once or twice when accompanying her aunt Veronica to the real estate office. She had not seen him in the present day in which she could identify him conclusively. "Evidently, someone wants this investigation shut down. But what if it wasn't Dillman who came after me and threatened us both? After all, my initial belief was that the unsub may have been Zach Gilliard. That didn't exactly pan out. Maybe the hypnosis led to false memories."

"I doubt that." Scott regarded her intently.

"The fact that you were able to describe a bright red windbreaker with a hood that just happened to match one Dillman owned at the time, according to Jeanne Singletary, strikes me as much more than pure coincidence. Combine that with the other elements that lend themselves to Dillman being a serious suspect and the contentions here simply cannot be ignored."

"You're right." She met his gaze and put a fork to the moo goo gai pan. Coincidences and criminality did not typically go hand in hand. "Seems like Oliver Dillman has some major explaining to do, if totally innocent, past and present. But would he really shoot my aunt to death merely because she rejected him?"

"Wouldn't be the first time that's happened," Scott replied matter-of-factly, sitting back. "Some people refuse to take no for an answer and turn rejection into a personal affront that could lead to deadly consequences. Beyond that, Dillman and Veronica worked together and there could have been some animosity there on Dillman's part that caused him to lose it in targeting her. And then you, two decades later, for fear of recognizing him when the investigation got too close. We won't know for sure till we see if the pieces fit into place and can bring him in."

"Okay." Abby drank water thoughtfully. "I'd just like it over, one way or the other."

"It will be soon, I promise," Scott said in a way that made her believe him.

"And what about us?" She threw it out there, feeling the need to. "Where do you see things going?" *I may as well lay it on the line*, Abby told herself, wanting to know if there was a future between them. Or was it all in her head?

He looked her right in the eye and answered without prelude. "I see them going as far as we can take what we've been given." Scott tilted his face. "I'm into you, Abby, and want nothing more than to let things play out between us, with no holding back."

She swallowed thickly. "I feel the same way."

He grinned, leaned over, kissed her as though to prove a point and uttered smoothly, "Good."

Abby flashed her teeth, feeling a tingle of excitement. She believed that no matter the outcome in the cold case investigation, things between them gave her real reason for optimism. Something that had eluded her when it came to relationships in the past. Scott had proved to be cut from an entirely different cloth. She was seeing that more and more with each passing day.

And found herself giving back as much, accordingly.

THE FOLLOWING MORNING, Scott saddled up the horses and they went riding. Abby seemed almost as much a natural on the American Cream Draft horse as he was on his Thoroughbred. He saw that as another sign they truly were on the same wavelength. As last night would attest to when they'd made love like there was no tomorrow. Of course, he believed there would be many more days ahead for them to cultivate what they had started. He wasn't about to allow Oliver Dillman or any other unsub to come between him and Abby, preventing them from giving themselves the opportunity to find the lasting love they both so richly deserved.

"It's breathtaking out here," Abby commented as they rode across rolling hills.

"I agree." Scott smiled, thinking of how cute she looked wearing Annette's cowgirl hat. If he had his way, one day she would be riding with a hat of her very own. "But if the truth be told, you take my breath away even more."

She giggled, blushing. "Ever the charmer."

"Is it working?" he teased her.

"I'll let you figure that one out all on your own."

Scott laughed. "I'll take that as a yes."

"Smart man." She beamed. "Race you back to the barn."

"You're on." He loved this playful side of her,

probably as much as the other qualities that made Abby the woman she was. "But don't take it too personally if I win."

"I won't, if you don't," she quipped, and took off.

Scott gave her a generous head start before directing his horse, Sammie, to go after Abby, while pushing away for the moment the cold case that continued to be a thorn in their sides.

Chapter Fifteen

Two days later, Scott was in his office when he received a video call from Cynthia Salazar.

He accepted and gazed on the laptop at the KentuckyFam forensic genetic genealogist whose short dark brown hair had light blond balayage ombré highlights. "Hey," he said.

"Hi, Agent Lynley." Cynthia fixed him with green eyes behind geometric gold glasses. "I have news for you."

He sat back. "I'm listening."

"Okay." She took a breath. "Utilizing information you gave me, I was able to construct a genealogical profile of the crime scene unknown male DNA profile," she said evenly. "Turns out there was a rather large family tree with DNA submitted to genealogy databases that corresponded with the unknown suspect's DNA. It resulted in a very close DNA match with a man named Walter Dillman, who gave his saliva to a genealogy project. I did some digging and learned that, though Mr. Dillman died twelve years ago, he did have a son..."

"Oliver Dillman," Scott guessed.

"Bingo!" Cynthia's face lit up. "Though your murder suspect has never used a genealogy service, he might as well have," she argued. "Given the other correlates you have on him, I'm betting that once you get his DNA, it will be a match with the unknown male DNA profile from the car at the crime scene."

Scott grinned. "I have a feeling you're right," he stated instinctively. "Send me everything you have and more!"

"Will do."

"Good work, Cynthia."

She blushed. "I love my job and being able to assist in cold case criminal investigations. Hopefully, this can lead to an arrest and conviction of Veronica Liu's murderer, Agent Lynley."

"I'll let you know how it works out," he told her and said goodbye.

When Scott presented his case half an hour later to Diane Huggett, the assistant special agent in charge in the Louisville field office, he was practically bursting at the seams in his desire to compel Oliver Dillman to submit a DNA sample. And, in the process, almost certainly linking it to the DNA an unsub left behind at the crime scene, before or after Veronica Liu was shot to death.

"All the signs point toward this guy," Scott insisted, standing on the opposite side of his boss's credenza desk. "Dillman's got guilt written all over him. Including a strong likelihood that he is the unsub who attacked my chief witness in the investigation of Veronica Liu's murder, her niece, Abby Zhang."

Diane leaned forward in her blue task chair and said, "You present a convincing argument, Lynley."

"I was hoping I would." He maintained a serious look.

"I'd love to see this case solved. Especially for that little girl who is now a great asset for the Bureau's Victim Assistance Program."

"Couldn't agree more." Scott could almost taste the joy this would give Abby to close the case with an arrest and conviction. She deserved at least that much, if not much more. "I'll need that search warrant to get Dillman's DNA, for starters."

"You've got it." Diane's eyes twinkled. "I'll get on the phone with Judge Helen Urich."

Scott nodded and was now tasked with going after Oliver Dillman and possibly encountering resistance from the murder suspect.

"I HAVE A search warrant to get Dillman's DNA on record," Scott told Abby over the phone. "It's the first major step in learning once and for all if the unidentified male DNA profile belongs to him."

"Really?" She was in her office when taking the call and elated with the news.

"Yeah. KentuckyFam and the forensic genetic genealogist came through in finding a very near match of Dillman in his late father."

"Wow." Abby had always been curious about her own family tree, wondering how far back she could go to get a genetic roadmap that led to herself. Her parents and grandparents had given her snippets of their genealogy. But that had only left her wanting to know more. Maybe when this cold case investigation was over, she would pursue that in earnest. And perhaps, even talk Scott into seeing who'd come before him and his more immediate family. "I have a good feeling about this, Scott." To feel otherwise would be like practically giving up on identifying her aunt Veronica's killer. Abby would never do that, so long as the case remained open.

"Same here. Of course, the proof is in the pudding, as they say. Or, in this instance, the DNA."

"Very true." She chuckled. "At least you aren't

giving Oliver Dillman a choice in turning over the DNA."

"Not a chance!" Scott made clear. "I'd say that the man has run long enough from his past. It's high time it caught up with him."

"Amen to that," Abby said, her voice betraying the need to have closure in this dark place in her life.

"I'll keep you informed on how things turn out."

"I wouldn't expect any less."

"Catch you later."

"Definitely," she told him, going beyond the common phrase and thinking in literal terms about spending time together and what it could signify beyond that.

Afterward, Abby briefed Elodie Zimbalist and then, with the accompaniment of the FBI agent, rendezvoused with Victim Services Coordinator Elise Martinez for a crisis intervention in Hancock County. Only, the agents had averted the crisis at the last moment. So instead, Abby took Elodie and Elise out for lunch, happy to have connected with two women in the Bureau she could call friends.

WITH HIS GLOCK 17 GEN5 MOS placed firmly inside the shoulder gun holster, and in possession of a search warrant, Scott left Murlock

Realty Group, where Oliver Dillman worked, having been told that he hadn't come in that day.

Hope he hasn't skipped town, Scott ruminated as he hustled back to his Ford Explorer. He wouldn't put it past Dillman to make a run for it. Especially if he felt the walls were beginning to close in on him.

Scott decided that it was more likely that Dillman had simply chosen to take the day off. Perhaps dealing with a hangover. Or maybe he was stalking another woman, believing he was out of the woods as a murder suspect, fresh off his latest warning to back off the investigation. Whatever the case, Scott took solace in the fact that Agent Zimbalist was keeping an eye on Abby, and would be ready to go into action should any trouble arise.

Putting his cell phone on speaker and placing it in a dashboard holder, Scott made arrangements for agents from the Owensboro FBI office to meet him at Dillman's house on Circle Court. In the meantime, Scott barreled toward the location, believing there was not a moment to waste here. Desperate people were prone to desperate acts. Before he was onto them, Scott wanted to get Dillman's DNA on record and act accordingly should it prove to be a match with the unknown crime scene profile.

When he arrived at the ranch home on a cul-de-sac, Scott waited for backup while noting that there was no sign of Dillman's silver Lexus UX 200. He considered that the car could be parked in the garage. Or, his number one suspect in the murder of Veronica Liu could be anywhere right now.

When the agents showed up, ready and willing to do their part for a colleague in Abby by taking down Dillman, if necessary, Scott made his move. He identified himself and banged on the door, calling out to Dillman while demanding that anyone inside open up. Just as it appeared that there may be no one home, the door opened.

A slender thirtysomething African American woman, with an Afro that had a shaved undercut, stood there glaring at them with big sable eyes.

Flashing his badge, Scott told her, "FBI Special Agent Lynley. I'm looking for Oliver Dillman."

"He's not here," she claimed, full lips pursed. "Who are you?"

"Shannon Emmanuel. I'm Oliver's girlfriend."

Scott cocked a brow with the age difference. "Where can I find Dillman?"

"I have no idea." Shannon hunched her shoulders. "He didn't come home last night."

"Mind if we come inside?" Scott asked. "We need to make sure you're being on the level with us."

"Be my guest." She parted the way and the FBI agents went in and fanned out.

Scott remained standing with Shannon in the open-concept living area with traditional furnishings. "Does Dillman often stay out all night?" he questioned.

"Sometimes," she confessed. "He likes his own space. And I respect that, since I feel the same way. It's what makes this work."

"I see."

"Clear," an agent shouted, indicating that no one else was present. Least of all, Oliver Dillman.

So where is he? Scott asked himself, fearful that Dillman had taken off upon sensing that they were onto him. "Why don't we have a seat?" he told Shannon. She complied, sitting on a track armchair, while he sat on the leather sofa. "When did you last speak to Dillman?"

"Last night about eight," she replied.

"Did he say where he was?"

"A bar. He didn't tell me which one. I didn't ask."

Scott brushed the tip of his nose. "Did he indicate that he didn't intend to come home last night?"

"No. But Oliver doesn't always let me in on his plans." She sighed. "So, what's this all about anyway? Why does the FBI want to talk to my boyfriend?"

"Dillman's a person of interest in a cold case investigation," he told her straightforwardly.

Her eyes widened. "You mean murder?"

"Yeah, I'm afraid so, which is why we need to find him. Do you have any clue as to where Dillman might be?"

Shannon started at the question and answered, "I wish I did." She paused. "He could be with another woman. Oliver is prone to stray every now and then, but since we aren't exactly exclusive, that's his choice."

Scott decided this was as good a time as any to get to the real root of the visit. "I have a search warrant to collect Dillman's DNA." He presented it to her. "As the man is absent, I'll have to get his DNA in another way." Scott stood, inviting her to as well. "I need you to show me his razor or toothbrush."

Shannon rose and led him to the bathroom, pointing to the objects in question. Scott donned a pair of nitrile gloves and gathered the suspect's toothbrush and a razor that had a few hairs stuck to it. He placed them in an evidence bag.

Now we need to get this to the crime lab in

a hurry to see what they come up with, Scott told himself anxiously.

At the front door, he handed Shannon his card with his cell phone number and said, "If Dillman shows up, tell him the FBI needs to reinterview him as soon as we can arrange it."

She glanced at the card. "Okay."

Outside, Scott got on the phone and issued a BOLO for Oliver Dillman and his silver Lexus.

WHEN KOLTON LAKE PD Homicide Detective Selena Nunez got word that a man had been found shot to death in a Lexus UX 200 in an isolated section of Kolton Lake Park, she headed straight to the crime scene. Another day in the life of someone who had spent the last two decades dealing with death. It was never easy to lose people. Even those you didn't know. But, at least, if within her power, she would try to get to the bottom of it for the loved ones left behind.

Arriving in her duty vehicle, Selena parked behind a squad car with its lights flashing. She got out of the car, showed her identification to the tall, bald-headed male officer at the scene, and said to him routinely, as if clueless, "What do we have?"

"A deceased male," he told her. "Apparently

died by a self-inflicted single gunshot to the head, with the weapon on his lap."

"Hmm…" Selena frowned. Too many people chose to check out that way these days. Never giving themselves a chance to see if there just might be a better tomorrow. Next week. Or next year.

She approached the vehicle and, after putting on latex gloves, opened the driver's-side front door and took a look inside. The decedent was slumped against the steering wheel. From what she could make out, she guessed him to be in his late fifties. A gunshot wound was in his left temple. Blood had spilled out onto his yellow shirt and khaki pants. Selena noted the firearm, resting precariously on one leg. She leaned forward, studying the gun. It looked to be a Colt Python .357 Magnum revolver. "Do we have a name for the deceased?" she asked the officer.

"I ran the license plate," he answered characteristically. "The car is registered to an Oliver Dillman."

Oliver Dillman. Where had she heard that name? Selena contemplated this for a long moment before it clicked.

As she recalled, Dillman had been one of the suspects in the murder of Veronica Liu twenty years ago, but had been given a pass when circumstances suggested he wasn't the killer. Now he had apparently offed himself. Coincidence?

Or could there be some symmetry here between the past and present? She called in the Crime Scene Investigation Unit to come collect and preserve evidence of a potential crime.

Just then, Selena got a message over her radio, indicating that a BOLO had been issued for Oliver Dillman as a person of interest in a cold case homicide.

Chapter Sixteen

Scott received word that Oliver Dillman had been found dead in his car in Kolton Lake Park, with preliminary indications that it was suicide. This was troubling in the sense that Scott would have preferred to interrogate the murder suspect and, if found guilty, see to it that Dillman spent the rest of his miserable life behind bars. Instead, the death short-circuited that plan and all was now within the jurisdiction of the Kolton Lake Police Department.

When he arrived at the death scene, Scott took a moment to study the decedent, who was still in his car, and mused about the irony of how he died in relation to Veronica Liu's murder in her vehicle. Was this justice served? Or more like justice denied?

Detective Selena Nunez approached and said to him bleakly, "Looks like our cases have intersected, Agent Lynley."

Scott grimaced. "Yeah, seems that way, Detective. Or maybe it's more that this thing has come full circle for you," he remarked thoughtfully.

"I admit, it does give me the déjà vu heebie-jeebies," Selena uttered. "Having Dillman reenter my orbit again two decades later does catch my attention."

"Any chance that someone could have offed him and made it look like a suicide?" Scott had no reason to believe this, given that Dillman had emerged as his prime suspect in the cold case murder. But all bases needed to be covered.

"Always a chance, though not very likely by all appearances," she told him. "The firearm apparently used, a Colt Python .357 Magnum revolver, was on Dillman's lap prior to being bagged by the CSI Unit for evidence. No indication as yet that anyone else was at the scene when it happened. We're checking out surveillance video in the park to see the comings and goings in this area."

Scott looked at her with reaction to the gun make and model, in particular. "Did you say it was a Colt Python .357 Magnum revolver?"

Selena met his regard with a perceptive nod. "I know what you're thinking. Same thing entered my head. It's the same type of firearm as the gun used to shoot to death Veronica Liu," she recalled. Her brow wrinkled. "Hard to conceive that this is, in fact, the murder weapon, still in service. But as we were able to recover a shell casing at the scene that we think came from the Colt Python .357 Magnum, ballistics will make a clear determination on whether that's true and if it was the same handgun in both shootings, along with the ammo comparisons between the two shootings."

"Good." Ideally, Scott would've preferred that the evidence be turned over to the FBI Laboratory, but he had no real authority to take over her current case, which was well within the Kolton PD's jurisdiction to investigate. Still, he hadn't counted on Dillman keeping the murder weapon around two decades later. What were the chances of that? And, if true, actually using it to shoot himself to death? *Maybe*, Scott considered, *Dillman's suicide was his way of redemption or giving them what they needed to close the case.* He asked the detective curiously, "Did Dillman happen to leave a suicide note?"

"Not that we've been able to determine thus far," she said. "But then, as you know, that isn't always the case. Sometimes, a despondent person decides on the spur of the moment to end it all, and leave everyone to question why."

"Yeah," Scott allowed. But was that actually what had happened here? Or was it possibly made to look like the man had taken his own life? "Having Oliver Dillman check out like this complicates my investigation somewhat," he confessed, not comfortable with some still-unanswered questions.

"I can imagine." Selena ran a hand through her hair. "Heard that you put the BOLO out on Dillman. Obviously, you had good reason to believe he was the unsub or had crucial information in Veronica Liu's murder?"

"You could say that, on both fronts." Scott glanced again at Dillman's dead body, knowing he would remain that way till the medical examiner arrived. "Pending verification, I think it was Dillman's DNA that was left on Veronica Liu's vehicle. Other factors also lead me to believe he was the culprit in her death. I'm guessing that he knew we were onto him and, when faced with a long stint behind bars, chose to take the easy way out."

"Appears that way." Selena angled her face. "If so, we'll be able to close the books on two cases at once, making both of our lives a little easier."

"Yeah, we'll see if it works out that way." Scott had been around long enough in law enforcement to know not to get too far ahead of himself in any investigation. Least of all, one that had been anything but cut-and-dried for the past two decades. Yet he clung to the notion that Dillman's death could put this to rest and give Abby the closure she needed, once a couple of other things fell into place.

"OLIVER DILLMAN'S DEAD?" Abby gasped as she gazed at Scott's solemn face in her log cabin.

"The early indications are that Dillman killed himself as we were closing in." Scott was holding a glass of wine while standing near the living room windows overlooking the lake. "We'll know just how true that is once the autopsy is completed."

She batted her lashes musingly. "What about my aunt Veronica's murder?" Abby could only hope that Dillman's death wouldn't put that into a deep freeze all over again.

"We'll get the answers we need there, too, soon," Scott stressed. "We have Dillman's DNA and fingerprints to compare with the unidentified ones found at your aunt's crime scene. Beyond that, the firearm we believe Dillman used to take his life was a Colt Python .357 Magnum revolver, the same type of weapon used in Veronica Liu's murder. It's a good chance that this is the very same gun that, against all odds, Dillman chose to hang on to. It's being examined by the Kolton Lake PD's Ballistics Laboratory, even as we speak."

"Okay." Abby sipped her wine. "So, we hold our breath till then?"

Scott touched her cheek. "We trust the system to do its job," he said steadfastly. "The rest will take care of itself."

She nodded thoughtfully, even as Abby wondered about the rest, as it pertained to their lives after the case was officially closed. Having Scott so near, she had practically forgotten what it was like to not have him around. She was sure that whatever else happened, they would continue to be a part of each other's lives. All that remained was to what extent. She looked at him now, trying to read his thoughts and wondering if they synchronized with hers on where this was going between them when all was said and done.

THE BRECKINRIDGE COUNTY Medical Examiner and Coroner's Office was located in Hardinsburg, Kentucky, seventeen miles from Kolton Lake. Scott met Selena Nunez there the following morning once news came that the autopsy on Oliver Dillman had been done, with both seeking definitive answers.

Greeting them in the examination suite was Chief Medical Examiner Daryl Fujimoto, MD. In his midforties and thickset, he had black hair in a buzz cut, a thin goatee, deeply lined brown eyes, and was wearing surgical garb. He gave nods and said, "Agent Lynley. Detective Nunez."

"Hey, Doc," Selena said.

Scott acknowledged him and asked without delay, "So, what can you tell us about the cause and manner of Oliver Dillman's death?"

Fujimoto sighed then answered in an even tone of voice, "You can check out the full report when it's ready, but I can tell you that Mr. Dillman's death was caused by a direct-contact single gunshot to the left-side temple. With no obvious signs of foul play—and none pointed out to me, along with the decedent confirmed to be left-handed—in my opinion, his death was almost certainly self-inflicted."

"Had Dillman been drinking?" the detective asked curiously. "Or otherwise under the influence of something?"

"The decedent's blood alcohol level was almost three times the legal limit," Fujimoto responded matter-of-factly. "I've ordered toxicology tests to further determine if, and to what extent, there were any drugs in his system that may have played a role in the death. If only the decedent's state of mind."

Scott listened intently as Fujimoto spoke, seeing little reason to doubt the findings, in light of the police investigation. But there was still more he needed from the pathologist, for further clarification. "What was the estimated time of death?"

"I'd say sometime between nine and midnight the night before last," he responded candidly.

Scott mused about his questioning of Dillman's girlfriend, Shannon Emmanuel, who'd claimed she had last spoken to him around 8:00 p.m. Had his plans been in place then? Or had this been an impromptu act? Or neither?

Scott asked Fujimoto, "Did you happen to test Dillman's hands for gunshot residue?"

The medical examiner rubbed his goatee and replied, "I did at that, given that Mr. Dillman was under criminal investigation, making GSR testing mandatory."

"And…?" Scott gazed at him anxiously.

"Using a scanning electron microscope, along with energy-dispersive X-ray analysis, the tests came back positive for some traces of gunshot residue on the decedent's hands. Though this could have technically come from putting them up in a defensive manner or residual GSR, when coupled with the other factors, it makes the conclusion that this was self-inflicted that much more likely."

"Works for me," Selena stated. "Seems like Dillman's violent past finally caught up to him in what, honestly, was a long time coming, if I'm reading the tea leaves correctly."

Scott, too, had to go along with this, considering. At least, at face value. But he was keeping an open mind on Dillman's untimely demise, till being able to effectively link it with the remaining pieces of the puzzle as they pertained to the murder of Veronica Liu.

DETECTIVE NUNEZ'S ASSUMPTIONS about Oliver Dillman's history picked up steam in Scott's mind, validating his own discernment as he accompanied her to the Kolton Lake PD's Ballistics Laboratory. There, Gregg Borelli, a firearms examiner, had tested the weapon and ammo connected to Dillman's death and compared it with the .38 Special cartridge and casing used in Veronica Liu's murder.

Borelli—who was in his thirties, lean and around six feet tall, with long and slicked-back brown hair in a man bun—gazed at them with blue eyes, as he told them at his workstation, "I think I have what you're looking for..."

Scott regarded him. "Go on."

"Okay. After test-firing the Colt Python .357 Magnum revolver found at the scene of Oliver Dillman's death, I compared it with the .38 Special cartridge Dillman was shot with and the casing recovered. The ammo was both fired from the same gun barrel with four lands and grooves with a right-hand twist, and the ballistic markings on the casings were a perfect match with the cartridge removed from Dillman's head."

"Suspected as much," Selena told him. "Now, what about the .38 Special round used to kill Veronica Liu?"

Borelli's face lit up. "We're talking about the same weapon used," he said confidently. "I compared the .38 Special cartridge and casing used in the Liu murder to the ammo in the Dillman shooting, and the two were totally in sync and shot from the Colt Python .357 Magnum revolver recovered from Dillman's vehicle."

"You're sure about that?" Scott asked, if only to hear him say it for the record, given the implications.

"Yeah, I'm sure." Borelli's face hardened. "This is what the Kolton Lake PD pays me for. You can have the FBI crime lab verify my findings, but they won't be any different. The same firearm was used in separate shootings spanning two decades."

And presumably with the same shooter, Scott realized, assessing the forensic ballistics info as measured with the autopsy results on Oliver Dillman. This still left the results of the DNA testing and unidentified partial print found at the crime scene to nail down Dillman as the shooter in Veronica Liu's cold-blooded execution.

ABBY MAY HAVE jumped the gun a bit, but she couldn't resist meeting with Jeanne Singletary for lunch at the Twenty-Second Street Bistro in Kolton Lake to share the news about the cold case that they both had been burdened by for two decades. Though Abby had invited Elodie Zimbalist to join them, her soon-to-be ex-FBI bodyguard had chosen to give them their space and was sitting at a nearby table, on her cell phone for presumably her next assignment.

"The investigation into Aunt Veronica's murder may finally be coming to a head," Abby said as they sat in a booth with mugs of hot coffee and lunch menus between them.

Jeanne's brow lifted. "Really?"

"Yep. Looks like your read on Oliver Dillman and his bright red hooded windbreaker has yielded positive results," she told her. "Well, maybe not so much the jacket, per se, but the man who was wearing it." Abby sighed. "Dillman's dead."

"Dead?" Jeanne regarded her with shock, nearly spitting out her coffee.

"Yes. Apparently, he took his own life the night before last," Abby said, knowing it was public knowledge by now. "There was a BOLO out by the authorities to bring him in for questioning and to collect his DNA in connection to Aunt Veronica's death."

"And rather than man up, he chose to escape being held accountable for a despicable act of murder by killing himself?" Jeanne's mouth hung open in anger.

"Sure looks that way." Abby was outraged as well. She would have much preferred that Dillman face her and Jeanne in court for his heinous actions before having to pay for his crime by imprisonment.

"The Bureau still needs to tie up a few loose ends, but Scott and Kolton Lake PD Detective Selena Nunez, the original investigator on the case, seem to believe he's the culprit. Including recovering the murder weapon and linking it to Dillman." It was still astounding to Abby that he had not bothered to get rid of the gun before deciding to turn it on himself. But then, she couldn't exactly get into the head of a killer and the choices he made.

"Well, if this can finally give Veronica the long overdue resting in peace that she deserves, so be it," Jeanne declared, glancing at her menu.

"That's true, I suppose." Abby was not about to look a gift horse in the mouth. But she wasn't quite ready to pronounce victory either. Not until Scott felt he had enough to close the case for good.

Jeanne smiled at her. "Why don't we order?" she suggested. "I, for one, am starved and the food will go down much better with your news of the day. And maybe I'll order something a little stronger than coffee to help wash it down."

She smiled back at her aunt's best friend and business partner. "Yes, let's have lunch." Abby lifted her menu and looked to see what was best, having regained her own appetite as she contemplated what may lie ahead.

Chapter Seventeen

Scott was in his car on the laptop when Federal DNA Database Unit Laboratory Scientist Kay Nakata and the Bureau's crime lab's Latent Print Unit forensic examiner Matt D'Angelo appeared on the screen.

After updating them on where things stood in the investigation, Scott favored Kay with a direct look and watched her face brighten as she said, "Yay to KentuckyFam. Had a feeling they might be able to help in this cold case."

Scott grinned. "They did come through," he reiterated, wondering if she would do so, as well, when asking the lab tech in earnest, "What do you have for me on the DNA comparison?"

"I have great news, Agent Lynley." Her white teeth shone. "In comparing the DNA samples you provided from the suspect, Oliver Dillman, to the unidentified male DNA profile taken from the Mercedes-Benz belonging to murdered victim Veronica Liu, I'm happy to say it's a match!"

"Really?" Scott asked routinely, but had no trouble believing her.

"Absolutely," Kay asserted. "The DNA belongs to the very same person."

"Oliver Dillman?"

"Yes," she stressed. "Of course, I'm not the one to say that he murdered Ms. Liu, but he did definitely leave his DNA on her car, for one reason or another."

I can think of only one solid reason, Scott told himself, piecing this with the other solid and circumstantial evidence that correlated with Dillman's involvement in the homicide twenty years ago and his own death. "That's good enough for me," he affirmed. "The fact that Oliver Dillman was at the crime scene when he wasn't supposed to be, and has now suddenly taken himself out of the equation, tells me pretty much all I need to know."

"Makes sense," Kay uttered.

Scott gave Matt the benefit of his attention, wondering if he had been able to match the latent print from the car with Dillman's left index finger, on the off chance that it would somehow be a hit, in spite of Dillman's prints being on file as a licensed real estate agent. "What did you come up with on the print comparison, out of curiosity?"

D'Angelo pulled on his beard and said levelly, "I examined the print from Oliver Dillman's left index finger and put it under the microscope to see if it miraculously lined up with the unidentified person's left index finger latent print. As expected, they were not a match."

Scott nodded accordingly. "Had to try."

"My guess is the partial print left on the car was unrelated to the homicide," D'Angelo suggested. "It most likely was put there at some other time by someone else who knew Veronica Liu. Or who came into contact with her vehicle by happenstance."

Kay agreed, arguing, "Frankly, I'm surprised there weren't even more unidentified latent prints left on the car. Between family, friends, coworkers, auto repair personnel, vehicles are like a magnet for finger and palm prints."

Scott did not disagree. Only in this instance, they were able to account for all prints on Veronica Liu's car other than this one. If it didn't belong to Dillman, could there have been someone else involved in the murder? There was no evidence to support this angle, Scott realized, but more than enough to believe that Oliver Dillman acted alone in shooting to death Abby's aunt.

D'Angelo broke into his thoughts when he said, "Since I had Dillman's prints, I ran them through the Next Generation Identification system just for the hell of it, to see if anything came up."

"Did anything?" Scott asked, wondering if Dillman could have previously run afoul of the law and it had been missed.

D'Angelo shook his head. "Not a thing. Looks like, apart from the homicide in question, Dillman managed to keep his nose clean through the years."

There was the attack on Abby. Scott believed that Dillman was most likely the unsub, having the most to lose with her possibly identifying him, were the investigation to continue. The fact that he had chosen to take his own life wouldn't let him off the hook. "I think I have what I need to pin the murder of Veronica Liu squarely on Oliver Dillman's shoulders," Scott told them assuredly. Now he needed to convey this to Abby, the person with the most vested interest in having the right conclusion necessary to put the case to rest.

LATE THAT AFTERNOON, Abby was walking with Scott along the sandy shoreline of Lake Kolton. Both were barefoot and glancing periodically at the lake, mesmerized by the sun's rays reflecting off the smooth surface of the water. She was being briefed about the state of things in the investigation into her aunt Veronica's murder.

Abby listened attentively as Scott told her fluidly, "Oliver Dillman's DNA matched the unidentified male DNA profile left on your aunt's car. When you add this to the fact that the Colt Python .357 Magnum revolver and ammo Dillman used to kill himself was forensically matched with the murder weapon and .38 Special cartridge used in Veronica Liu's death, we have our killer."

Abby was almost speechless trying to put into words the elation she felt now that her aunt's murderer had been officially identified for the whole world to see. "So, it's over then?" she dared to ask, gazing up at him with expectation.

A grin played on Scott's lips when answering coolly, "Other than a little paperwork and a sign-off by the assistant special agent in charge in the Bureau's Louisville field office, Diane Huggett, and the Kolton Lake PD, the original law enforcement agency investigating the homicide? Yeah, I'd say this case can finally be closed with a satisfactory outcome."

Abby showed her teeth. "Thank you, Scott, for all your hard work in taking this seriously." She felt as though a tremendous weight had been lifted off her shoulders. "I once feared it would forever go unresolved."

"I couldn't have done much of it without your help, Abby," he told her, voice lowered in expressing his sincerity. "Without your dedication to your aunt and holding on to some crucial details inside your head, waiting to be released under the right circumstances, Dillman might have forever remained under the radar."

She thought about the bright red windbreaker he'd been wearing the day of the murder and how it had somehow stood out within her subconscious mind for two decades. Had Dillman not seen her as a real threat, which may never have actually been the case, in attacking her at the park that day, the truth could well have stayed hidden for all time.

"I'm glad I was able to contribute in a small way," she uttered modestly. "I only knew that Aunt Veronica was there for me when no one else was. I needed to return the favor."

"And you did," he promised her. "On some other plane, I think she knows that."

Abby nodded and suddenly realized that Scott's long arm was territorially across her shoulders as they continued to walk on the shoreline. She liked the feel of this and wondered if it was a sign of things to come now that they had crossed one major bridge on their journey.

THE NEXT DAY, Scott was at work, finishing up what was needed in the Veronica Liu cold case, eager to put it behind him and move on to new cases sitting on his desk. He admittedly hated leaving Abby's log cabin after staying the night. Moreover, he hated having to be away from the gorgeous victim specialist at all. But if he had his way, that wouldn't be a problem for too much longer as he looked ahead. He intended to ask Abby to marry him. Yes, they hadn't known each other a superlong time by conventional standards. So what? Knowing someone for a longer period of time hadn't exactly worked in his favor previously.

Scott sat back, dismissing the short span of their romance. *When you know, you just know that someone's right for you and you're right for them*, he told himself. Waiting wouldn't change that. It would only make it more frustrating living their lives apart. If Abby accepted his proposal, they could work out the logistics later.

His cell phone rang and Scott saw that the caller was his brother, Russell. Answering, he said easily, "Russ."

"Hi. Just checking in to see how your latest cold case is coming along."

"Funny you should mention that." Scott smiled out of a corner of his lips. "As a matter of fact, I was just able to solve the case."

"Why am I not surprised?" Russell laughed. "Guess that's why the Louisville Kentucky FBI field office doesn't want to let you go. They damned well know a great cold case agent when they have one in their midst."

Scott chuckled while eating it up. "Back at you, little brother, in holding down the fort in the Bureau's Houston field office."

"So, give me the short story on who the unsub was and how you cracked the case."

"Okay." Scott did just that, sparing him the tedious details about going after Oliver Dillman, while playing up the involvement of Abby Zhang.

Russell remarked, "Sounds like you two made a great team."

"More like make a great team," Scott corrected him, knowing his brother would demand more. And he was happy to oblige.

"Hmm...am I missing something here?" Russell's voice lowered an octave. "Have you been holding back on us?"

"Not exactly." Scott thought about having confided in Annette that he was interested in Abby romantically. His sister had apparently kept it under wraps, allowing him to spill the beans in his own good time. Now was as good a time as any to get started on that score. He finished with, "I'll let you know how she responds when I pop the question."

"You're full of surprises, Scott," Russell told him wryly. "And that's why I love you, big bro. Never a dull chat."

"Works both ways." Scott chuckled. "Later."

No sooner had he disconnected when his phone rang again. Scott didn't recognize the caller as he answered in his professional voice, "Agent Lynley."

"Agent Lynley," the man said unevenly, "my name's Elliot McGowan. I'm an attorney based in Kolton Lake, representing the recently deceased Oliver Dillman."

Scott reacted, wondering why Dillman's lawyer would be contacting him. "I'm listening."

"We need to talk," McGowan said in vague terms. "Can we meet?"

If only out of curiosity alone, although his interest was piqued by more than that, Scott felt he had no real choice but to accept meeting with the dead man's attorney.

IN THE MORNING, Abby revisited some crime victims as part of her duties and to make additional referrals, where needed. Afterward, she headed over to Kolton Lake General to meet her friend Dr. Phoebe Hoag for lunch in the cafeteria.

Abby got off on the third floor in search of

Phoebe and, after heading down the hall, instead found herself nearly running into Zach Gilliard. Though he seemed almost as shocked to see her, Abby had to ask him suspiciously, "Are you following me?"

"No." Zach's thick brows knitted. "Absolutely not!"

She remained wary. "So, why are you here?"

"I was visiting a friend," he claimed, stuffing his hands in the pockets of his cargo pants.

She rolled her eyes. "Yeah, right."

"It's true. I'm not stalking you, Abby. I swear." Zach made a face. "After that FBI Agent… Lynley…warned me in less than a subtle tone to stay away from you, I got the message and have tried my best to do so. Even if I never felt I did anything wrong by simply sending you thank-you roses and having a brief chat at the cemetery."

"Okay, I get it." In spite of wondering if she may have overreacted where it concerned him, Abby was happy that Scott had applied pressure in getting Zach to back off, in spite of his not having made any overt threats. Or having been guilty of shoving her to the ground at Kolton Lake Park, with Oliver Dillman proving to be the perp. Her instincts told her that Zach could still have been a problem, had he been given an opportunity for his interest in her to escalate.

He took a breath. "Anyway, sorry we almost ran into one another. My bad."

"It's no one's fault," she told him, and meant it.

Zach nodded, stepping aside. "I'll let you go wherever you were headed."

"Same." Abby met his eyes briefly, unsure what to make of him, but eager to be on her way. "Goodbye, Zach."

"'Bye, Abby." After a moment, he walked away.

She watched him for a few seconds before heading in the opposite direction, where she spotted Phoebe.

Her friend, wearing a white lab coat, approached her. "Sorry I'm a little late."

Abby smiled. "No problem."

Phoebe glanced over her shoulder. "Who was that man you were talking to?"

Without bothering to look his way again, Abby replied with a sigh, "It's a long story."

Phoebe cupped her arm. "You can tell me all about it over lunch."

"SOUNDS LIKE A creep to me," Phoebe remarked fifteen minutes later as they sat by the wall in the cafeteria.

"Maybe Zach's just misunderstood or lonely," Abby suggested, trying to give him the benefit of the doubt that she may have misread his gratitude toward her.

Phoebe wasn't buying it. "Isn't that how all stalkers get started in the wrong direction, by just *seeming* lonely and misunderstood?"

Abby gave a little chuckle while lifting her turkey grinder. "Believe me, I'm not trying to cover for him," she insisted. "But as a victim specialist, I can't let those I help get to me, any more than some unruly or unsettled patients who might become fixated on you."

Phoebe smiled. "Point taken." She bit into her club sandwich. "Guess some things come with the territory, like it or not."

Abby concurred. "In any event, Scott has warned Zach to stay away and he seems to be abiding by that."

"That's good," Phoebe said and ate more of the sandwich. A moment later, she looked across the table at Abby and asked curiously, "So, what's happening with you and the FBI agent these days?"

Abby put her sandwich back on the plate and dabbed a paper napkin to her mouth. "As a matter of fact, that's what I wanted to talk to you about, in a manner of speaking..." she began, and then sprang the news on her about the case of her aunt Veronica's murder being solved at last.

"Seriously?" Phoebe tilted her head to one side. "Tell me more."

"A guy named Oliver Dillman, who used to work with Aunt Veronica, who rejected his advances, apparently shot her to death in a jealous rage, I suppose," Abby told her, and sipped iced tea.

"Oliver Dillman?" Phoebe's mouth gaped. "Isn't that the real estate agent who took his own life the other night at Kolton Lake Park?"

"That's him," she told her.

"I read about it." Phoebe paused. "So, he killed himself because the FBI had figured out what he did to your aunt twenty years ago?"

"Sure looks that way." Abby tasted the tea. "The gun Dillman used to kill himself was the same weapon that was used to murder Aunt Veronica. The ammo between the shootings matched up as well."

"Wow." Phoebe drank her black coffee. "This is so unreal."

"I know." Abby sighed. "As it turns out, I actually saw Oliver Dillman right after it happened as he ran off into the woods."

"What?" Phoebe's jaw dropped. "Why am I just hearing about this?"

"I never realized it till undergoing hypnosis recently," she admitted to her. "You knew I saw something out in the woods as I got to

Aunt Veronica's car. Though I never got a good look at a face, the hypnosis revealed that it was a man wearing a bright red windbreaker with a hood. According to my aunt's business partner, Jeanne Singletary, one matching that description was worn by Oliver Dillman. Scott was about to connect the various dots before pinning the murder on him."

Phoebe shook her head in astonishment. "How did he get away with it for so long?"

Abby lifted her hands in equal disbelief. "Same way others have gotten away with terrible crimes over the decades, even centuries," she reasoned. "By being clever enough to conceal their identities, keep the authorities guessing, and by refraining from committing similar crimes."

"I suppose you're right." Phoebe took a breath. "Thank goodness it's over."

"Yeah, it's a big relief." Abby couldn't begin to express just how much. Never knowing why someone went after her aunt Veronica had been a big drag on her own life. Now she could finally move on. Hopefully, with Scott.

As though reading her mind, Phoebe leaned forward and said, "You never did say where things are with you and Scott on the personal side."

"I didn't, did I?" Abby giggled.

"Well…?"

It took her a moment or two of contemplation before Abby looked her friend since childhood in the eye and told her, "I think I'm in love."

Phoebe's face lit up. "Seriously?"

"Yes." She couldn't deny what she was feeling, even to herself. "There's just something about Scott Lynley that has tapped into my emotions on a level I've not experienced before." *Not to mention he's a great lover.* Abby colored at the thought. "While he's been married before," she pointed out, "it wasn't the right fit for him or her, so I can't hold that against him in moving on. Any more than my own previous relationships that went nowhere."

"That's fair enough," Phoebe allowed, picking at the remains of her sandwich. "Most of us fail to get it right the first time," she conceded. "You think he feels the same way about you?"

Abby twisted her lips contemplatively. Did he? Or had she somehow read his expressions, tender words and body language all wrong? "Yes," she uttered. "But so I don't jinx things, I won't speak for him. We'll just have to see what happens." Or doesn't, she had to prepare herself for, whether Abby wanted to think in those terms or not.

Chapter Eighteen

Scott stepped inside the McGowan and Kusuda Law Offices in the Rellington Building on Ninth Street in downtown Kolton Lake. He wondered just what Dillman's attorney would be contacting him for, after the man was dead. *Guess I'm about to find out*, Scott mused as a young and thin, blond-haired female office assistant ushered him into a large, carpeted office with window walls and modern furnishings.

After she left, he was approached by a tall, navy-suited, medium-sized man in his late fifties with short, wavy reddish hair. Regarding Scott with deep gray eyes, he stuck out a hand and said casually, "I'm Elliot McGowan."

"Special Agent Lynley." Scott flashed his identification as such and met the attorney's gaze squarely while they shook hands.

"Thanks for coming."

"I admit being surprised to hear from a lawyer on behalf of Oliver Dillman," Scott said forthrightly.

"I understand where you're coming from, Agent Lynley." McGowan rubbed his crooked nose. "Why don't we sit down and I'll explain?" He pointed toward a guest lounge chair for Scott, while taking a seat in his own leather executive chair, behind a U-desk suite. McGowan sighed. "Mr. Dillman—Oliver—and I go back a long way."

"How long is that?" Scott asked, as though he needed to, while seated.

"Since we were teenagers. We both attended Kolton Lake High School back in the day and stayed in touch infrequently. I've been Oliver's attorney for probably ten years now, just normal dealings pertaining to legal advice on real estate transactions, investments, liabilities, that type of thing." McGowan leaned back in his chair before saying, "I was saddened to hear about Oliver's passing."

So was I, though likely for entirely different reasons, Scott told himself. He straightened his shoulders impatiently and asked the lawyer bluntly, "Mind telling me why I'm here?"

"Of course." McGowan leaned forward and pressed his hands against the wooden desktop. "Not long ago, Mr. Dillman handed me an envelope and requested that, in the event of his death, I was to give it to you, Agent Lynley…"

"Is that so?" Scott narrowed his eyes, mystified.

"Yep." McGowan opened a top drawer and removed a padded envelope. He slid it across the desk. "I'm fulfilling that obligation."

"Do you know what's in it?" Scott asked curiously before picking up the envelope.

"Have no idea," he claimed. "Oliver never told me and I never asked, out of respect for him as a client."

"I see." Scott lifted the yellow envelope and, feeling it, could tell that there was what seemed to be a smallish box inside. Whatever was within, he preferred to see what Dillman was up to alone. "Is there anything else you want to tell me about your client?" he asked the lawyer, wondering if any attorney-client privilege would be waived under the circumstances.

"Nothing I can think of," McGowan said. "Apart from my legal responsibilities regarding his estate, whatever Oliver felt he wanted to say to you is likely in that envelope."

"In that case, I think we're finished here," Scott said, getting to his feet before being told the same by the lawyer.

"Right," McGowan agreed, standing.

Scott accepted another handshake and was out the door. He waited until he was inside his SUV before grabbing latex gloves from the glove compartment. After putting them on, he tore open the envelope and removed the small box. Opening it, he saw that it contained a flash drive.

Is this Dillman's confession to murdering Veronica Liu? Scott asked himself. A virtual suicide note? Or both?

He lifted his laptop from the passenger seat and slid in the flash drive, watching as Oliver Dillman's face appeared and he began to speak.

ABBY FELT A bit nervous returning to the cemetery to visit her aunt Veronica's gravesite, recalling that Zach Gilliard had followed her there previously. But as she scanned the well-manicured grounds, there was no sign of the mass shooting survivor who had seemed infatuated with her. Or maybe she had been spooked by him for no good or bad reason. Whatever.

He shouldn't be a problem anymore, she thought, with Scott running interference for her. For which Abby was most grateful. Along with other reasons to be glad he was in her life.

She focused on her aunt's headstone and spoke to her aloud in a sentimental tone of voice. "It's finally over, Aunt Veronica. The man who took you from me has been identified and can no longer pose a threat to anyone else, ever again. You can now rest in peace eternally, and I'll do my best to forever keep you in my memory."

Abby took another cursory glance around the cemetery and spotted only an elderly couple, who seemed oblivious to her presence. She turned back to her aunt Veronica's grave and said a silent prayer, one that included being able to find the happiness that had eluded her aunt. Particularly when it came to romance and making the wrong choices in her life. In Abby's way of thinking, she had turned the corner in that respect and could see only promise and possibilities for what may lie ahead.

SITTING BACK IN his SUV's front seat, Scott was fully attentive as he watched Oliver Dillman speak to him from the grave.

"Hello, Agent Lynley. There's no sugarcoating it. If you're watching this now, it means I'm no longer alive. Since I'm sure you're a busy man, as I used to be, I won't take up too much of your time."

Dillman sucked in a deep breath and continued. "I made the mistake of first getting romantically involved with Freda Neville twenty-plus years ago. That was way before she would go on to become Kolton Lake Mayor Freda Myerson. Anyway, what was only playing the field for me was something altogether different for her. With a jealous streak a mile long, Freda mistakenly saw my coming on to my work colleague Veronica Liu as one competitor too many.

"Truthfully, I actually thought that Freda was pulling my leg when she swore she'd kill Veronica if she tried to come between us. The night before her death, I made the mistake of talking shop with Veronica when we ran into each other at the Tygers Club. It really set off Freda, who was there with me, in a way I hadn't seen before."

He drew a breath and Scott recalled the bartender and former exotic dancer Katlyn Johansson remembering the exchange between Veronica and an unidentified man. Scott had had no way of knowing at the time that this was Oliver Dillman. Much less that he'd been in the company of Freda Neville.

"Convinced that I was two-timing her with Veronica, Freda just lost it," Dillman stated. "She wanted to kill the person Freda thought was standing in the way of what we had. Next day, with Freda wearing my red jacket, I followed her to Veronica's cabin, still not believing she would actually commit murder."

Dillman sucked in another deep breath. Scott was jarred as he considered the bright red windbreaker that Abby had revealed under hypnosis had been worn by her aunt's ostensive killer.

Scott peered at the laptop screen as Dillman uttered in a shaky voice, "I watched as Freda shot Veronica while she was in her car. Then Freda took off for the woods. I went to check on Veronica, but could tell that she was already gone. That's when I saw her niece, Abby Zhang, walking down the street, heading toward the cabin.

"I hid behind the cabin and waited for her to see what she saw and go inside, before I took off running into the woods myself." Dillman grabbed a can of beer, drank a generous amount and then continued. "When I caught up to Freda, I tried to get her to turn herself in. But she threatened to implicate me in the murder—say we'd both planned it—if I didn't keep my mouth shut. What could I do?"

He threw his hands up, as if in surrender, and said, "Things were never the same for us after that. A little while later, we went our separate ways, with the secret still intact." Dillman drank more beer. "Stayed that way till you reopened the case, Agent Lynley. Freda was spooked that you would find out the truth and arrest her for murder, causing her carefully structured world to come crashing down around her. She warned me to keep a lid on it. Or else."

Scott contemplated all he had heard with incredulity as Dillman tasted more beer, burped and said, "Anyway, I got to thinking… I'd run into some money issues, bad debts, that sort of thing, and decided that Freda owed me. She agreed to the tune of one hundred grand and we could keep this thing buried forever. But first, I needed to get you to back off. Hence the text message warning on a burner phone. When that didn't seem to work, I came after Abby Zhang. I was never going to hurt her. Just scare her, so you'd drop the case and I'd get what I needed from Freda."

Dillman sat back and stared into the camera. "To be clear, I don't trust Freda. Not one bit, after what she did to Veronica. But being in real estate, I understand that everything's worth the risk for the rewards that come from it." He finished off the beer. "If you're watching this, it means my lawyer handed it over as requested, in the event of my death. And it would only come if Freda chose not to hold up her end of the bargain and I ended up paying for it with my life. If that's the case, it tells you all you need to know, Agent Lynley, about just what Freda is capable of and willing to do to Abby Zhang. Next time you talk to Abby, give her my apologies about what happened at the park. And, of course, the death of my former colleague Veronica Liu."

The video ended, leaving Scott visibly shaken. Especially when it came to fear for Abby's safety. No matter how this played in sorting out the facts of presumably fingering the wrong unsub in Oliver Dillman, in spite of the direct and in-direct evidence to support the contention, Scott knew that, if everything Dillman confessed to was true, Abby's life could be in grave danger. With her enemy, Mayor Freda Myerson, hidden in public view. And Abby's new role with the Crime Victims Advisory Board only a smoke screen for the mayor to keep an eye on her, hop-ing Abby didn't remember it was Freda she'd seen running in the woods the day Veronica Liu was murdered, and not Oliver Dillman.

Scott doubted it would take much for Freda to want to eliminate the last threat to her cushy life and political aspirations, even with Dillman now out of the picture.

I can't let the mayor add Abby to her list of killings, Scott asserted determinedly, closing the laptop and setting it back on the seat. The love of his life would not become another vic-tim of homicide. He took out the cell phone from his pocket and called Abby, needing to warn her about Freda.

There was no answer. Scott typed Abby a text message.

Abby. Oliver Dillman may not have killed your aunt. His ex-girlfriend Mayor Freda Myerson appears to be the guilty party. Stay away from her. Call me ASAP.

He sent it off and then headed over to Abby's log cabin, sensing that she needed him now as much as he needed her. Before Freda Myerson could end what he and Abby had ahead and what they were building upon in the special way they both deserved.

AFTER ARRIVING HOME, Abby turned off the security system and took her cell phone upstairs to charge. Back downstairs, she went into the kitchen to pour herself a glass of wine. She took a sip and thought about where things would go from here, now that her aunt Veronica's murder had been solved. Abby believed that there was a future to be had with Scott and that both would pursue this, even if their past relationships had soured them as far as happy endings. The past was certainly not always a barometer of the future. Nor should it be, other than using it as a learning experience for a better outcome down the line.

Abby kept that thought in mind as she thought she heard a sound. Then there was a knock on the door. She hadn't been expecting any guests, but considered that her friends Phoebe and Beverly were prone to dropping by uninvited. Putting her wineglass on the counter, Abby walked to the door. She looked out the peephole and was surprised to see that it was Freda Myerson. The mayor was wearing casual clothing, which included a dark hoodie.

Without giving it another thought, albeit curious, Abby opened the door. "Mayor… Freda…"

"Hello, Abby." She showed her teeth. "Did I catch you at a bad time?"

"No, not at all." Abby smiled back. "Come in."

Inside, Freda faced her and said, "I was in the neighborhood and thought I'd take a chance you were home to discuss more about the Crime Victims Advisory Board."

"I'm here," Abby quipped. "And I'd be happy to talk about my role with the board. Can I pour you a glass of wine? I have coffee and tea as well."

"No thanks." Freda stared at her. "So, I understand that Agent Lynley was able to close the case on Veronica's death by identifying Oliver Dillman as the killer?"

"Yes, that's true." Abby was thoughtful. "All the evidence, such as Dillman's red windbreaker, which I saw him wearing the day Aunt Veronica was killed, pointed to Oliver. Including the murder weapon, which he also used to take his own life. How weird is that after holding on to the gun for two decades?"

"Pretty weird," the mayor agreed. She paused for a long moment before saying distantly, "Problem is, Abby, Oliver wasn't the one you saw wearing the hooded red jacket. It was me."

"What?" Abby met Freda's suddenly cold eyes with confusion. "I don't understand."

"Oliver and I were dating at the time," she stated coolly. "I wore his jacket as a show of affection. Or, at least, it began that way. I thought he was the love of my life. Or wanted him to be, if only Oliver didn't have such a wandering eye. One that paid far too much attention to Veronica Liu, who seemed just as infatuated with him as I was. At the time, I was very much the jealous type and took it personally when someone tried to steal what was mine. Very personally."

Abby gulped in asking, ill at ease, "So what are you saying?"

"You're smart, Abby. Figure it out." Freda waited a beat. "It was me who shot and killed your aunt. Not Oliver."

"You—" Abby's voice broke as she weighed this stunning admission.

"That's right." Freda's face tightened. "He was much too weak to do anything like that.

Honestly, I wonder now what I ever saw in the man. At the time, though, I felt Oliver Dillman was someone I wanted to spend the rest of my life with. Silly me. Anyway, I intended to be in and out after waiting in the woods for your aunt to arrive home. I made sure she knew it was me who was about to take her life before I pulled the trigger. I left her there to die and thought I'd made a clean getaway. Then I looked back and saw you had come home from school a little sooner than anticipated. I was sure we'd made eye contact and actually thought about coming out of the woods and killing you too. But it was too risky at that point and I took off.

"When you never mentioned this to anyone and were sent away to be with relatives in San Francisco, I thought I was in the clear." Freda snorted. "But in the back of my mind was the fear that you just might remember seeing me and my house of sand would come crumbling down around me."

"I never did remember seeing you, Freda," Abby admitted, her heart beating wildly while trying to come to terms with the fact that Mayor Myerson had just confessed to murdering her aunt Veronica. How had she come to believe the person she'd seen that day under hypnosis was a male? Why couldn't she have gotten a close look at the killer to see her for who she really was?

"And maybe you never would have, Abby. Problem is, even with Oliver dead and identified as the shooter—giving me the cover I needed to get away with it forever—I simply cannot afford to take that chance." On that note, Freda removed a handgun from the pocket of her dark-colored hoodie. She pointed it at Abby and said tersely, "It's loaded."

Abby stared at the firearm. She recognized it as a Taurus G2C 9 mm Luger. "You're going to kill me?" she blurted out.

"I'm afraid I don't really have much choice, Abby." Freda's voice fell an octave. "I've come too far to see my life as mayor of Kolton Lake and wife of a brilliant man in Pierce Myerson, who actually gets me and accepts me for who I am, be potentially ruined by something that happened two decades ago."

I need to somehow buy time, Abby told herself as she stood there. She had no way of knowing if Scott had possibly figured this out or not. Even if he had decided that Oliver Dillman wasn't the culprit after all in her aunt's death, Abby doubted Scott would be able to ride in on his Thoroughbred horse, Sammie, to save her from the mayor. *I have to find a way to come out of this alive*, Abby thought, knowing that any future she might have with Scott had suddenly been put in serious jeopardy.

She regarded the mayor hotly. "Oliver Dillman didn't take his own life, did he?" Abby had a feeling, in spite of the conclusions drawn by the medical examiner and authorities.

"Not exactly." Freda gave a derisive chuckle. "Seriously, I thought that Oliver and I were through twenty years ago. But then, just like that, he came waltzing back into my life when the cold case was reopened. When he should have simply left well enough alone, instead, Oliver tried to hit me up for one hundred grand." Her nostrils flared. "Or, in other words, the man was blackmailing me in order to keep his mouth shut for something he caused to happen way back when by two-timing me with the likes of Veronica. And who knows how many other women?

"Well, I would have none of it then," she hissed, keeping the gun aimed at Abby, "and I certainly wouldn't allow Oliver to control my life now!" Freda sighed. "So, yes, I killed him with the very gun I used to shoot your aunt. Wisely, I thought it was a good move to hold on to it as an insurance policy, in case I needed it again. I agreed to meet Oliver at Kolton Lake Park in an area that I knew was remote and had an escape route. He foolishly agreed to this, believing he would pocket the hundred grand and maybe use me as a forever piggy bank to fuel his excesses. That was his fatal error in judgment."

Stunned by all this, Abby's mouth became a straight line as she voiced, "So you set him up to make it look like a suicide, while planting the revolver that you knew would implicate Oliver Dillman in my aunt Veronica's death?"

"Brilliant, wasn't it, if I say so myself." Freda laughed humorlessly. "Why not kill two birds with one stone, so to speak. I allowed Oliver to think he'd succeeded in getting the payoff, then followed him back to his car, where I shot him at point-blank range with the very same Colt Python .357 Magnum revolver I shot your aunt with, and strategically placed it on Oliver's lap. With him being seen as Veronica's killer, it let me off the hook. Except for the fact that you present a final loose end that could someday come back to haunt me for past sins. I can't allow that to happen, Abby."

She cringed in horror. "You'll never get away with this, Freda."

"I've heard that before." The mayor chuckled nastily. "Something tells me I will get away with it—again." She pointed the gun's muzzle at Abby's face. "Why don't we take a little walk?"

"To where?" Abby's eyes narrowed with suspicion.

"Not far," she claimed. "Out in the woods, where you'll have a fighting chance to escape unharmed. If you do, then I'm toast." She laughed, waving the gun threateningly. "But I must warn you, Abby, I've become a pretty good markswoman with enough target practice over the years to know how to make it count when my mind is made up."

With her arms folded defiantly across her chest, as if to stop incoming bullets, Abby challenged her. "And what if I refuse to leave the cabin?"

"Then I'll simply shoot you in the face right here and now!" Freda asserted. "Don't test me." She tightened her grip on the firearm. "What's it going to be, Abby?"

As if she needed to think about it, Abby took only a moment before responding firmly, "I'll take my chances out in the woods."

"Thought you might." The mayor grinned crookedly. "Let's go."

Abby glanced around the cabin, looking for anything she might grab to hit her with. Though she spotted an item or two that might do the trick, with Freda laser-focused on her and brandishing a gun, Abby saw no benefit in making a courageous last-second stand. Only to come up short.

And in the process, lose any chance of surviving her aunt Veronica's killer in Freda Myerson, and having a life with Scott Lynley. Those were odds that Abby wasn't willing to take as she headed out of the cabin, with her whole world on the line.

Just as was the case with the mayor, who was once again playing this game of cold-blooded murder for keeps.

Chapter Nineteen

Scott was still trying to wrap his head around Oliver Dillman's long-winded but telling confession after his own death to being a party to Veronica Liu's murder, albeit after the fact. While pointing the finger squarely at his ex-lover Freda Neville, now Mayor Freda Myerson, as the real culprit in the death of Abby's aunt. Including being the one who was wearing the hooded bright red jacket instead of Dillman. Presumably, the unidentified left index fingerprint found on Veronica's Mercedes-Benz had no bearing on the case, per se, beyond clearing others along the way.

All things being equal, Scott had no reason not to believe the pre-deathbed confession of a man who chose to lay it all out on the line in the name of a blackmail payday. Only to pay the ultimate price with his life. If so, that was on him, as greed and opportunity often made for a bad combination. Especially when pitted against a cunning killer who was more than willing to take out anyone who stood in her way.

That included Abby, much to Scott's chagrin.

When he arrived at her cabin, having already called for backup, he spotted Abby's Subaru parked in the driveway. No sign of another vehicle that may have been driven by Freda Myerson. Not that he would have expected the mayor to show up with her own car. Much less an official vehicle with a driver. Still, Scott wondered if his instincts that she might have come after Abby were way off base. Especially since Myerson could not have known that Dillman had left a recorded video message in the event of his untimely death.

Once out of his SUV, Scott headed toward the cabin, when out of the corner of his eye, he spotted movement in the wooded area. Peering in that direction, he saw two figures. One was definitely Abby. The other was someone wearing a hoodie. That person appeared to be holding a gun and directing Abby to walk. Then, suddenly, Abby began to run, as if told to do so.

It didn't take putting two and two together for Scott to realize that the one holding the gun, presumably Freda Myerson, fully intended to shoot Abby in the back. Head. Or wherever. And then probably make an escape to a car waiting for her on the other side of the clearing. Whereupon she would resume her mayoral duties and get on with the life she had carved out for herself with her past buried for good.

Not happening, Scott determined at the thought of such an unwanted scenario. He whipped out his Glock pistol from the holster and took off. Then he heard a shot ring out. And another. His heart skipped a beat as he raced into the woods, praying that he wasn't too late to save the woman of his dreams and, hopefully, future wife and mother of their children.

ABBY DID NOT believe for a moment that she was capable of outrunning a bullet. Much less two, three or four fired by a maniacal mayor intent on covering her murderous tracks. But desperate times called for desperate measures. Or, in this instance, called upon her skills as a jogger and her awareness of the wooded area outside her log cabin to try to evade a sure destiny with death, were she to give in to it.

Before the first shot could even be fired, even with barely a head start, Abby had put into motion a plan to zigzag to the point of near exhaustion in confusing the shooter, while strategically using the dense black walnut and yellowwood trees as cover. It was apparently working as she heard one shot and then another, neither hitting the mark as Abby measured her breathing while managing to avoid becoming the fatal victim of a killer's target practice.

Then Abby heard the sound of a familiar voice say in a demanding tone, "FBI! Mayor Myerson, drop the weapon. Now! Or so help me, you won't make it out of the woods alive!" A moment later, a shot was fired away from Abby, followed by another shot, before she heard Scott say concisely, "I won't allow you to escape justice through suicide by cop."

Abby knew that this was in reference to those who try to compel law enforcement to use deadly force against them while shying away from self-inflicted death. Turning around, she could see Freda Myerson lying on the ground and Scott standing over her, kicking away the gun from the mayor's outstretched hand.

With it all seemingly happening in a blur, Abby found herself pivoting and racing back to the man she loved and her would-be killer. When she got there, she saw that Freda had been shot in the shoulder and was moaning in pain, but didn't appear as if she was at death's door.

Scott put away his gun and wrapped his arms around Abby, and asked her tenderly, "Are you hurt?"

"No. Guess today was my lucky day, sort of,"

she told him shakily. "The trees acted as great cover for flying bullets."

"Yeah, I can see that." He separated them and took out his cell phone, where he called 9-1-1 and reported the crime and Mayor Myerson's being shot.

Afterward, Abby gazed up at him curiously. "How did you know about Freda...and what she had planned for me?"

Scott sighed and answered, "Oliver Dillman left me a video message to be delivered by his attorney, should Dillman meet with foul play. In it, he incriminated the mayor as the one who actually shot your aunt in a jealous rage and roped him into helping to cover it up. Or be accused as participating in the murder. I texted you to warn you about her."

"I had my phone charging upstairs when Freda unexpectedly showed up at the cabin," Abby explained.

"Oh. Myerson was the one you saw wearing the red windbreaker that day," Scott informed her.

"I know," Abby uttered sadly, glaring at the mayor, who seemed to be drifting in and out of consciousness, no longer a threat. "Freda admitted it while practically gloating about coming after my aunt in her misguided vindictiveness over something that was never true.

The mayor also confessed to seeing me at the same time I saw her in the woods and had actually thought about finishing me off, as well, but chickened out. Thank goodness for that."

Scott gazed at her, asking in earnest, "What else did the mayor have to say?"

"That after Oliver Dillman tried to blackmail her, she tricked him into meeting her at Kolton Lake Park, where the mayor fatally shot him with the same Colt Python .357 Magnum revolver Freda shot Aunt Veronica with, and then planted the firearm on him to make it seem as though he had killed himself." Abby took a breath and wrung her hands as they trembled. "The entire thing is almost too much to believe."

"Yeah, it is." Scott pulled her to him. "But it's over now, Abby. Neither Freda Myerson nor Oliver Dillman, who also confessed to attacking you at the park to get me to shut down the investigation so he could sponge the mayor for money unabated, can ever hurt you again. And at least for the mayor, she will pay for what she did to your aunt Veronica Liu."

"I'm happy to know that," Abby stated, her voice breaking. "It's all I ever wanted." Or, at least, she'd thought it was. Up until Scott had entered her life. She stood on her toes and kissed him. "Now I want something more."

"So do I." He grinned charmingly. "So much more."

"How much is that?" she challenged him.

"Enough to make you my wife," Scott said boldly.

She raised her brows playfully. "Oh, really?"

"Yeah, if you'll have me," he reiterated. "I know the timing sucks, with us fresh off the cold case and still needing to deal with the mayor over there, but I'm in love with you, Abby, and for that, there's no time like the present to ask you to marry me and have a great life, including bringing children into the world as an extension of us." He drew a breath. "So, what do you say?"

Between rapid beats of her heart, Abby replied affectionately, "I say that if you hadn't asked me to marry you, I would have asked you to marry me. I've fallen in love with you, too, Scott, and yes, I'd love to become your wife and mother of our future children."

"Then consider both a done deal," he declared, "with a few steps along the way to bring it to fruition. Starting with this…" He planted a solid kiss on her mouth.

Abby parted her lips ever so slightly as she was all in with the kiss. She managed to put aside for the moment that they were standing in a forested crime scene, with her aunt Veronica's killer probably taking it all in with envy while facing a bleak future of her own making.

Unlocking their lips, Abby tasted the sweet kiss and told Scott devotedly, "That is a good start to a lifetime of happiness."

The huge grin on his handsome face told her he didn't disagree one bit.

Epilogue

Six months later, Scott sat in a Louisville federal courthouse, where the trial was underway for Freda Myerson. The former Kolton Lake mayor had been charged with the murders of Veronica Liu and Oliver Dillman, and the attempted murder of Abby Zhang Lynley, a witness aiding an FBI cold case investigation. Having recovered from a bullet wound to the shoulder and recently served with divorce papers by her husband, Pierce Myerson, the defendant looked less than confident in her chances of acquittal.

With good reason, Scott believed as he contemplated the strong case against Myerson on all charges. In the murder of Veronica Liu, there was Dillman's taped indictment of his former lover. The Colt Python .357 Magnum revolver she'd used in the homicide was traced through the ATF's NIBIN to an imprisoned drug dealer named Pablo Rodrigues, who was prepared to testify to selling the handgun to Freda Neville more than twenty years ago. Moreover, the former exotic dancer Katlyn Johansson was also a scheduled prosecution witness in claiming to have seen Neville with Oliver Dillman at the Tygers Club the night before Veronica Liu had been gunned down, establishing a link between the couple.

Scott glanced at US District Judge Craig Redcorn. In his early sixties, the Shawnee husband, father and grandfather had fine silver hair and sable eyes behind round glasses. The nononsense judge was always in control of his courtroom. Musing about the brazen murder of Oliver Dillman that Myerson was accused of, Scott considered the smoking gun, so to speak, or murder weapon that could be traced back to her. Then, there was the Kolton Lake Park surveillance video that showed a blue Nissan Murano, registered to the former mayor as her private vehicle, leaving the park near the remote area where Dillman had been found shot to death in his car. A reasonable inference could be made that the two former lovers had met one final time before only one walked away, according to Myerson's confession to Abby.

Scott's thoughts were interrupted by a text message on his cell phone. It came from his cousin Gavin Lynley, who was a special agent for the Mississippi Department of Corrections

Investigation Division's Special Operations and Major Crimes Units. Gavin wanted to pass along some good vibes in the successful prosecution of the object of Scott's cold case investigation, Freda Myerson.

Scott grinned in appreciation, knowing that his cousin, close to all the Lynley siblings, always had his back. And vice versa. He thought about Abby's impending testimony, as well as his own, against Myerson, who'd tried to shoot Abby to death in broad daylight. And might have succeeded, had Abby not been so quick and clever enough to zigzag just enough to throw her would-be killer off balance, while also using the trees themselves to Abby's advantage. This clear case of attempted murder was, to Scott, perhaps the strongest of the pretty persuasive cases against the former mayor. But no matter what happened, he intended to always be there in support of his wife and mother of their unborn child.

As if on cue, Scott turned as the prosecution called its star witness to take the stand. Abby Zhang Lynley. He watched as she entered the courtroom. She was as gorgeous as ever in a stylish chambray shawl-collar skirt suit and black pumps. Her long hair was worn in a cute twisted updo. They made eye contact and he mouthed silently to her to get up there and do what she needed to help put her aunt Veronica's killer away.

Scott sat back and took a breath while awaiting Abby's chance to finally exorcise the demons that Freda Myerson had brought upon her life.

ABBY GLANCED AT Scott and smiled as she sat in the witness box, representing them both as a witness for the prosecution. Not just as professional colleagues for the FBI. But as husband and wife. And, now two months pregnant, a mother-to-be to their first child, for which she couldn't be more elated. Being with the man she loved, and about to start a family, was all Abby could have asked for. Well, if all had been right with the world, she would have also asked that her parents and Aunt Veronica, as well as Scott's parents, could have been there to see them tie the knot. Since that hadn't been possible, Abby intended to count her blessings as they were.

That included the forces that fell into place to bring her to this moment in time in which she was being called upon to make sure that the former Freda Neville paid dearly for the bad things she had chosen to do against anyone who got in her way.

Abby had the expected butterflies in testifying against a woman who had pretended to be contrite in the death of her aunt Veronica Liu but in fact felt gleeful that her aunt was dead by Freda's own hand. Turned out that the invitation to become part of the ex-mayor's Crime Victims Advisory Board had been nothing more than a smoke screen for Freda to hide behind while keeping a close eye on Abby, should she get too close to the truth.

You won't get away with what you've done, a voice in Abby's head told Freda in earnest as she gazed at the defendant, who shot her back a cold stare. *There's nowhere else for you to hide from your terrible choices as a human being, Freda*, she thought candidly.

Abby regarded Naomi Bloom, the assistant US attorney, who was just a few years older than her, tall and slender, with long straight hair in a blunt cut and parted neatly in the middle. Naomi flashed her small blue eyes at Abby and said softly, "You'll do fine."

Abby nodded with that show of confidence, and took a breath before being asked a few identification-related and lead-up questions. Then she was asked about her memories of the day her aunt Veronica was murdered. Almost feeling as though she was under hypnosis again, Abby was drawn back to when she was twelve years old in recounting the moment she'd stepped off the school bus and headed the block away to her aunt's cabin. Seeing her inside the car, Abby confessed that her first thought had been that her aunt Veronica had simply fallen asleep, with her often working long hours.

It was only when she'd seen her up close, Abby testified, that she'd realized something was very wrong. Her aunt had not been moving and was bloodied. Abby had sensed that she was no longer alive.

Sighing deeply, Abby took a moment when Naomi readdressed her to talk about the person Abby had seen running off in the woods. Though she admitted to never getting a clear look at the killer's face, it was the bright red hooded windbreaker the suspect was wearing that stood out, seared into Abby's memory. She knew that Jeanne Singletary would testify later about a jacket matching this description that belonged to Oliver Dillman, Freda Myerson's ex-boyfriend, which Abby testified that Freda admitted to wearing the day she'd shot to death Veronica Liu.

By the time the testimony moved forward to the present and Freda's attempt to murder her as an unaware witness to a violent crime more than two decades ago, Abby had warmed up and was more than ready to take it to the disgraced former mayor of Kolton Lake.

Naomi Bloom positioned herself strategically on one side of the witness box as she asked Abby coolly, "Mrs. Lynley, why don't you walk us through that day six months ago, when you received a most unexpected visit from Mayor Freda Myerson…"

Abby looked Freda squarely in the eye and said succinctly, "I can do that." She proceeded to describe every moment of the encounter, in which Abby had seen her life flash before her eyes, as Freda had confessed to perpetrating two murders and her full intention to commit a third, with Abby the victim.

"With my life on the line," Abby recalled, "I honestly feared that Freda Myerson would succeed in her deadly plans for me, with the former mayor bragging about her marksmanship. At that point, all I could do was run for my life in the woods and hope for the best." She drew a breath and gazed first at her diamond contour wedding ring in 14k rose gold with round diamonds, then at her husband, Scott, who favored her with his handsome crooked grin. "Had Agent Scott Lynley not arrived when he did and stopped Freda in her tracks, I'm certain I wouldn't be sitting in this courtroom right now. And the ex-mayor might still have her old job. But things found a way to work out when they least seemed possible."

The assistant US attorney seemed more than satisfied with the testimony and finished up with a few more pointed questions and follow-ups. Abby then had to endure a withering cross-examination from the defense, for which she didn't falter, before she was excused. She left the witness box, feeling confident that she had given it her all in making the case against the defendant, before Abby was joined by Scott and they walked out of the courtroom, hand in hand.

"You knocked it out of the park," he told her cheerfully.

"Really?" Abby met his penetrating eyes. "You think so?"

"Of course." Scott smiled. "You were ready for this and delivered. Freda Myerson is toast and will pay for it."

"I'm glad to hear you say that." She stood on her tiptoes, cupped his cheeks and kissed him on the mouth. "Let's go home, darling," Abby said of their ranch, with her having sold the log cabin and, with it, finally putting to rest many unsettling memories.

He kissed her this time and, wrapping his arm around her waist, agreed endearingly. "Yeah, let's, sweetheart."

Two weeks later, the trial ended with closing arguments. After less than three hours of deliberation, the jury came back with a guilty verdict on all counts. US District Judge Craig Redcorn imposed the maximum sentence of life in federal prison for Freda Myerson.

Overjoyed with the news, Abby felt at peace that the long arm of the law had finally caught up with Freda Myerson in meting out overdue justice for the killing of her aunt Veronica Liu.

Abby knew that she would have welcomed Scott with open arms as part of the family had her aunt lived, and took solace in this as she rode leisurely alongside her husband on their horses along the trail, while wearing her own cowgirl hat and feeling like she truly belonged there.

* * * * *